An Irish vet looks back
by Fergus Ferguson ©

An Irish vet looks back
  by Fergus Ferguson ©

An Irish vet looks back
  by Fergus Ferguson

An Irish vet looks back
by Fergus Ferguson ©

An Irish vet looks back
by Fergus Ferguson ©

Table of Contents

Contents

An Irish vet looks back
by Fergus Ferguson ©

About the Author

Fergus Ferguson grew up in Northern Ireland. After studying at Trinity College, Dublin, he graduated as a veterinary surgeon in 1965. Ferguson worked as a locum, in various parts, of England, Ireland and Wales, including owning his own practice. This provided him with the unique opportunity to observe the quirks and peculiarities of clients, together with the idiosyncrasies of their animals. This gave the author an exclusive chance to observe these interconnected series of veterinary anecdotes as his career developed. Fergus retired from veterinary practice in 1998, and is currently enjoying his retirement, taking the opportunity to put pen to paper in his beloved Devon countryside.

An Irish vet looks back
   by Fergus Ferguson ©

An Irish vet looks back
by Fergus Ferguson ©

Tullymuck

The last term of my final year at Trinity College, Dublin, had arrived.
I still did not have a job. The situation in Ireland that prevailed at
that time was that most veterinary practices were one-man bands.
Furthermore, the reality was that I did not have sufficient confidence
or experience to apply for a job running a single-handed veterinary
practice, especially as I had not passed my final examinations. The
eccentric, gaunt Professor of Parasitology had been graphically
describing all the minutiae of Diphyllobothrium latum - the fish
tapeworm of man. A Russian fisherman was reputed to have harboured one
of over forty feet in his intestine. Generations of veterinary
students asserted that the very popular Professor looked rather like a
tapeworm himself. Suddenly, just like a conjuror producing a rabbit
out of a hat, the Professor pulled a crumpled letter from his breast
pocket.
'Has everybody got a job?' he enquired. 'I have a letter here from an
old Trinity graduate - a Mr Billy MacCaskie. He has a very busy
single-handed practice in Tullymuck, County Down. He wants a locum to
run his practice during his holiday.' The Professor, who was slightly
cross-eyed, looked directly at me with his good eye over his half-moon
spectacles, 'What about you, Fergus? Are you fixed up yet?'
My heart sank. Did he really think I was capable of running a
veterinary practice single-handed? Since I had not even qualified, the
question of the dreaded final examinations loomed ever larger in my

mind. I knew from all the horror stories I had heard that this type of work would be no sinecure, especially for a newly qualified young vet. Like a lamb to the slaughter, awash with nerves, I reluctantly accepted the proffered letter from his hand, without demur. Alarmingly, the College wag, who was sitting behind me, commented: 'Fools rush in where angels fear to tread.' I felt many a true word was spoken in jest. Later that evening, just outside the safety of the secure walls of the College, I found myself inside the nearest green claustrophobic public telephone kiosk, contaminated with the normal permeating whiff of stale urine and stale tobacco smoke, reminiscent of a public lavatory. I made sure that I had the necessary Irish pennies that showed an eclectic mix of pigs, chickens and harps. I nervously lifted the telephone receiver and inserted the mandatory pennies into the metal slot. A friendly operator enquired if she could help. I asked her to put me through to Tullymuck 13. As I listened nervously for a voice to answer, finger poised to press button A, my mind wandered, trying to conjure up a picture of Tullymuck and the local vet. Then I remembered the number, 13. Can a number seriously be unlucky or was I becoming superstitious? Midway through the conversation, I discovered that it was impossible to say no to Mr Billy MacAskie, he had an answer for everything.

'Will you run the Practice in my absence, Fergus?'

I could not believe my ears. Was he actually being serious?

'I'll come if I pass my final examinations,' I replied, thinking that this could be a possible escape route for me.

'Ah sure, never mind about passing the auld exams, just come along anyway,' he blustered, belligerently.

'What about signing certificates?' I enquired, thinking that this might get me off the hook. 'For sure, one of the neighbouring vets will attend to all dese tings, so you don't have to worry, at all, at all, at all.' he berated me, relentlessly.

All my fears and protestations were swept aside with aplomb. There was no stopping him. In a futile attempt to reassure me, he continued, 'I'll have a good man waiting to help you. Sure, he's been helping my locums for years.'

Perhaps at this stage, alarm bells should have been ringing. What had become of all the previous locums over the past years? Why had no one apparently been willing to return to Tullymuck so this poor man could take a holiday with his wife and children? But no. I could feel myself being inveigled deeper and deeper into the quagmire, with no way out. I heard myself agreeing to work for him for three weeks - the last three weeks in July - whilst he and his family went to France. Looking back on it now, it is still a complete mystery to me how I ever managed to pass any veterinary examination - let alone the fearful finals. However, in the event, I did, the culmination of five years' work and play. On a beautiful July day, my extremely proud parents came to applaud their prodigal son, attired in gown and mortarboard, for the conferment of the Degrees. The entire Ceremony was conducted in Latin. No one, least of all the graduates, understood a word of the proceedings.

An Irish vet looks back
by Fergus Ferguson ©

The following day, I came down to earth with a resounding bump. My
sister, very kindly volunteered to drive her 'little' brother to
Tullymuck, to his first 'proper' job. As we approached the beautiful
Mourne Mountains, during the two-hour journey, I became increasingly
edgy. On our arrival, in the small market town of Tullymuck, just at
the foot of the Mourne Mountains, we enquired of a small group of men
standing in the square, where we would find the local vet. It was
obvious by their exchanged glances and sudden changed body language
that they all knew the answer to our enquiry. 'Sure he's only a couple
of gunshots up the mountain road on the left.' said one man
quizzically, as he indicated with his outstretched arm and finger. Sure
enough, the house and surgery were located just as the man had said. My
sister deposited me, together with my leather suitcase, halfway up the
lane.
THIS WAS IT!!! As she drove away, I stood watching the car disappear
back down the narrow lane in a cloud of dust. I asked myself, what had
I done? What had I let myself in for? What would befall me? THIS WAS
FOR REAL!
Turning around, Mr Billy MacAskie was impatiently waiting, chain-
smoking outside his surgery, positively chomping at the bit in his
eagerness to be away and start his holiday. Towering above me, wearing
a multi-coloured shirt, together with stone washed denim jeans, which
were clearly purchased by his wife to get him in the holiday mood. Mrs
MacAskie, short and round, was surrounded by a complete kindergarten of
children, as she secured the final suitcase to the roof rack, whilst
one gangly son was impatiently revving up the car engine. The Hillman
Imp was already bursting at the seams but somehow everyone still had to
be squeezed in.
I was brought back to reality as I heard Billy confidently declare,
'We're off to the South of France. Here are the keys to the surgery.
There is only the one call to do. It is written in the Diary. I'll
see you in three weeks' time. Any problems, ring this number,' as he
drew an empty cigarette packet from his jacket pocket and nonchalantly
scribbled a telephone number on it. Thrusting it into my hand, he
leapt into his car and they were off.
My courage deserted me as I watched the MacAskie family disappearing
rapidly down the lane, en route for the south of France, leaving me to
cope, totally alone, save for an almost indecipherable telephone
number. As I waved goodbye to them in a half-hearted, feckless
fashion, I could hear a telephone ringing from the depths of the
surgery - a never ending, expanding newish bungalow excavated into the
incline of a hill. Panic set in. What nightmare case awaited? The
ringing seemed to become louder and more insistent. There was nothing
for it, but to find the machine and answer it.
Unlocking the surgery door with trepidation, I tracked it down and
nervously, lifted the receiver, announcing myself to an unfamiliar
world, 'Tullymuck, 13.'
'Is that Mr Billy MacAskie, himself?' asked a deep menacing male voice
in a disingenuous manner. The farmer snarled, 'I've got a big cow
calving. There is nothing to feel but a tail. We've all tried to get

her calved but we're beat. My neighbour, Willy McCluskey has been
calving cows all his life and he's beat as well. If Willy can't get
her calved, there's only one man in the whole County who's fit for the
job and that's Mr Billy MacAskie, himself. What should we do?'
I was just about to say, 'If I were you I'd call the vet,' when I
suddenly realised - I WAS THE VET! My pulse was racing. My palms were
sweating. At this juncture, I wished that I had never become involved
with my chosen profession. I took a deep breath, and then tentatively
asked the farmer if he would like me to attend his calving case.
Reluctant to commit himself, he questioned me further, 'When will Mr
MacAskie be back?'
Hesitantly, I replied, 'In three weeks' time.'
On hearing this alarming piece of news, the farmer nearly exploded:
'She could be dead in three weeks.' Then, after a long pause, while he
was attempting to accept the reality of this unwelcome information, he
begrudgingly said, 'I suppose you had better come.' After a few
seconds of silent reflection, he bellowed, with aggression: 'Are you a
proper vet?' On receiving an affirmative reply, he continued, 'The
name's O'Sullivan from Upper Ballymucklekill.'
Without further ado, the telephone went dead. I realised that with a
townland name like Upper Ballymucklekill, it was sure to be a
terrifying mountain farm - a smallholding with no proper handling
facilities. I had no map. I did not know the district. What was I to
do? Why had I been so crassly stupid to agree to take on the
responsibility of this job - my first as a fully-fledged vet? I began
to realise my folly. Perhaps, with hindsight, I should have accepted
the safe, featherbedded, humdrum postgraduate research position in the
Department of Histology in the security of my Alma Mater.
The Professor of Gynaecology and Obstetrics had assured us that we
would have absolutely no problems finding farms. He had been a Colonel
in the Royal Army Veterinary Corps, where everything worked like
clockwork and happened with military precision. All vets would, of
course, be provided with the essential Ordnance map and the necessary
reference numbers by the practice principal. I can still hear the
Professor saying: "Don't forget the old Army aide-memoire - along the
corridor and up the stairs - to enable you to work out which three of
the six digits to read first." The Professor's words of wisdom seemed
vacuous and futile, and certainly did not appear to apply in the depths
of the Irish countryside, especially at Tullymuck. In desperation, I
suddenly remembered the empty cigarette packet with the barely readable
telephone number scribbled on it. What had I done with it? Pulling it
out of my pocket, I realised that this was my only guide. There was no
alternative other than to ring the mysterious number and see what
happened. Surely, things could only improve.
A warm, reassuring voice, with a local lilt as thick as the froth on a
pint of Guinness, answered the telephone, immediately making me feel a
great deal more confident. He seemed like an angel from Heaven.
'You must be Billy MacAskie's man. I have been waiting for you to
call.' The tone of his voice suddenly became conspiratorial. 'Sure,
between you, me and the gatepost, I always help Mr MacAskie's locums.

An Irish vet looks back
by Fergus Ferguson ©

I'm the local undertaker - Paddy MacCooey.' Consternation supervened
as I received this incongruous news. 'I'm rushed off my feet in the
wintertime,' he nonchalantly informed me, 'but in the summertime, 'tis
very slow. I stand around with my arms the same length. I have to
bury a good man tomorrow, but apart from that, I'm your man. Meet me
in the square in five minutes. You'll recognise me. I have a gammy
leg, so I walk with a stick.' What a bizarre combination, I speculated.
He sounded a most affable character who had certainly kissed the
Blarney Stone. Trust me to pick this practice, I thought, as I went in
search of the car keys to a Morris Oxford beach wagon - an appropriate
choice of car for Tullymuck. What a combination - a young vet and a
one-legged undertaker! The juxtaposition was manifest. Truth can
certainly be stranger than fiction. Would my contemporaries believe
me, I wondered, if I ever lived to tell the tale?

As agreed, I drove on to the square exactly five minutes after
replacing the handset. True to his word, the inimitable Mr Paddy
MacCooey was waiting, leaning on his stick, totally at home in this
typically Irish one-horse town. Recognising the motorcar, he hailed me
with a flourish of his walking stick; his face wreathed in smiles, his
blue eyes twinkling and full of mischief. I suddenly felt that I was
really going to enjoy these three weeks, now I had this wonderful
character to show me the way round the countryside and introduce me to
all the clients. My confidence was gradually growing.

Introductions and niceties over, the next task was to install Paddy.
It was quite a performance manoeuvring him into the passenger seat of
the car, together with his stiff leg, but well worth the effort. Paddy
knew the area like the back of his hand and, more importantly, knew all
the farmers and their families. He had buried generations of them.
What Paddy did not know about these farmers and their quirks, was not
worth knowing. Once ensconced in the passenger seat, Paddy pointed out
the farms and recounted all the gory details of previous veterinary
disasters, as we roared along the lanes. I tried to maintain my
equilibrium as he regaled me with further horror stories, but it was
all to no avail. Paddy could talk the hind leg off a donkey. He
seemed totally unaware of my apprehension and was more concerned about
what is known to all in the Irish countryside as "crack". For my part,
I was more concerned about steering a strange car to an unfamiliar
place, before the cow and/or the calf died.

As I drove up the rough, narrow, winding lane, which led to the top of
the beautiful Mourne Mountains and Upper Ballymucklekill, I felt
instinctively that, notwithstanding my inexperience and Paddy's rigid
leg, all would be well. Together we would make a formidable pair and
have a wonderful (or perhaps disastrous) three weeks, memories of which
would remain with me to the end of my days. The fantastic countryside
stretched as far as the eye could see. The magnificent Strangford
Lough, the biggest sea-inlet in the British Isles, could be seen in the
valley below. The loch is virtually totally enclosed by the Ards
Peninsula and is connected to the Irish Sea by a long narrow strait or
channel. It was a beautiful day in the height of summer. With this

trusty if somewhat unusual companion at my side, what more could a man wish for, I wondered.

As we drew to a halt in the ramshackle, disorganised farmyard, the place seemed awash with onlookers - a sea of strange faces, headed by the robust, sceptical figure of the owner, all eagerly awaiting our arrival, keen to see how Billy MacAskie's "man" would cope with the complexities of a difficult calving. Instinctively, this would be a make or break situation in this tight-knit community. Were all these different people a critical audience hoping for failure? It is always much more intimidating, particularly for a raw vet, to perform his professional duties in front of a much more experienced audience. News would travel very fast. It would be a baptism of fire. A case of derring-do. Where was my cow?

The stage was set. The metal bucket - full to the brim with hot water - together with soap and towel laid neatly to one side. Once led to my patient, who was standing straining in the stone byre, I was completely ignored. Everyone rushed to help Paddy extricate himself from the motor car. I was beginning to feel superfluous. I had very mixed feelings about this sudden change in atmosphere. It was a very definite double-edged sword. Paddy, who in many ways was probably my mentor, was centre stage, whilst I was an irrelevance, but I had to admit that I could not do without his invaluable help. I nervously donned my full-length plastic parturition gown in readiness for the delivery. As I dipped my hands in the scalding hot water, the skin nearly peeled off my fingers! Of necessity, a minute quantity of water, plus a liberal amount of disinfectant and lubricant were timorously applied to my hands and arms, in an unfamiliar and tentative manner, to enable me to prepare the cow's vulva for examination.

Before I had had a chance to give an opinion on the case, Mr O'Sullivan pontificated: 'You'll have to do a Caesarean operation vet, because we're beat!' The thought of effecting a difficult calving in the conventional way in front of an assembled audience filled me with horror, but the notion of having to perform a caesarean section (under duress) beggared belief. I would have much preferred to see if I could deliver the calf in the normal manner rather than be forced into performing a caesarean section on demand and perhaps against my better judgement, I thought.

Paddy hobbled over and grabbed the cow (a docile, dewy-eyed roan shorthorn) by the tail - positioning himself alongside the flank, so that we could converse privately. 'What do you feel?' enquired Paddy, encouragingly.

'I can feel the calf's backside and its tail,' I replied, nervously. 'I can definitely feel it moving.'

'Lord bless us, save us and take care of us,' said Paddy, with relief. In spite of all the previous unsuccessful attempts to deliver the calf, it was, miraculously, still alive. I knew that time was of the essence if the calf were to be saved. The cow's expression was anxious. I could feel her wince in pain. The presentation or position of the calf in the pelvis or birth canal was abnormal. Not only was the calf coming backwards but also, to make matters worse, both the calf's hind

An Irish vet looks back
by Fergus Ferguson ©

legs were extended straight forward. This abnormal birth position is known to the Profession as a breech presentation. Despite my lack of experience, I guessed that this was why the cow's periodic straining was to no avail. It also explained why all and sundry were bewildered. Normally they would expect to feel two front legs and a head but, confusingly, the only available appendage for them to feel was the calf's tail. This was not all. The foetal membranes or water bladder had ruptured some long time ago. The lining of the cow's uterus was very dry and swollen. This was due to the delay in calving and the several attempts at delivery. Confidently, I inserted a large volume of lubricant into the cow's uterus, in an attempt to replace the lost foetal fluid, thereby avoiding further trauma to the uterus and to facilitate the delivery, after this had been accomplished, my mind went blank. Having lubricated the cow's uterus, how was I to rectify the mal-presentation?

There was a nasty pause, seemingly endless, then like Manna from heaven the voice of my guardian angel, Paddy whispered reassuringly, 'The other vets usually push the calf's ass forward into the womb with one hand. They then slide their other hand down the calf's other hind leg and try to grab its hock joint. This enables them to follow the leg further down so that the fetlock joint can be caught and brought outside, ensuring she does not suddenly strain and push a foot through the wall of the womb.'

Invaluable information. It was just like the book (and the Professor) had said. I did exactly as I was bid and, to my amazement, it worked. One hind foot suddenly appeared from the cow's vulva. Paddy was in his element.

'What you have, you hold!' he pronounced, confidently. 'Now then, be a good man, fetch your rope and we're on the home straight.' Having safely looped the calving rope above the fetlock joint, so that the leg could not disappear again inside the cow's uterus, I looked to Paddy for further inspiration.

'You're on the pig's back now, Fergus. Just do the same thing on the calf's other hind leg and Bob's your uncle!'

With both hind feet safely held, Paddy, realising that he had a captive audience, knew he could now play to the gallery.

'All you need now, Fergus, are two good men, one to pull in turn on each rope, and everything will be hunky-dory. You just make sure the calf doesn't fall and hurt itself on the way out.'

Following Paddy's behest, innumerable enthusiastic spectators, who had been leaning against the walls cross-legged, instantly leapt forward; I was nearly trampled underfoot by the sudden stampede of willing helpers volunteering to pull on the ropes.

Now that the mal-presentation had been corrected, this somewhat bemused and long-suffering cow was, at long last, ready to play her part. Feeling that she needed some encouragement, I said, 'Come on, old girl - pooosh!' She gave an almighty heave and in the twinkling of an eye, the calf was delivered onto a welcoming bed of straw. Understandably, as a result of all the abortive interventions, the calf was not breathing.

An Irish vet looks back
by Fergus Ferguson ©

'Now Fergus,' said Paddy, 'throw a bucket of cold water over the calf
to try and make it breathe. This worked. The sudden shock of cold water
thrown on its head and flank made the calf gasp in an involuntary
reaction. 'Thanks, Paddy,' I said. Paddy's response was immediate and
helpful. "Now, stick a piece of straw up its nose that usually makes
the calf cough." I immediately selected a short piece of straw and
stuck it into the sensitive mucous membrane of the calf's nostril. The
calf instantly gave a hearty cough, clearing the offending mucus from
her lungs. I was in Paddy's debt yet again. "Now, release the chain
from the cow's neck. She'll do the rest for you with her tongue. By
the way, is it a bull or a heifer calf?' asked Paddy.
Happily, the calf - a heifer - was still alive. Slowly but surely she
tentatively started to breathe. The cow, with a watchful eye on the
gathering, proudly and enthusiastically, licked her newborn calf from
head to tail; instinctively knowing that all was well.
After witnessing that both cow and calf were going to be fine, Mr
O'Sullivan's face like thunder dramatically changed to one of sheer
delight, exclaiming, 'You're a grand man, vet. What did you say your
name was? You and Paddy deserve a cup of Tay. You'll be most
welcome.'
As Mr O'Sullivan led the way across the farmyard, followed by what
seemed to be a complete battalion of bystanders, I could see the smoke
coming out of the farmhouse chimney. Even though it was midsummer and
hay making time, the turf fires were constantly kept burning. In
anticipation of a large number of hungry mouths for tea, Mrs O'Sullivan
had positioned a large kettle full of water on the crook over the turf
fire in the kitchen. The smell of the burning turf and soda bread
evoked childhood memories of happy days spent at my uncle's farm in the
Derg valley in Co. Tyrone. The home-made soda farls topped with ample
lashings of butter and home-made jam - plenty for everyone - epitomised
Irish informal and spur-of-the-moment hospitality. Over half a century
later, I still remember the thrill of calving my first cow and Paddy's
invaluable guidance.
On my return to the surgery, I steeled myself to view the diary as I
wondered what Billy's mysterious 'only the one call' might be. The
problem about being a new graduate is that every single call is a
potential disaster. It is one thing to know everything in theory, but
putting it into practice is an entirely different matter, as I was
rapidly finding out. A glance at the diary confirmed my worst fears.
Scheduled for the next day - 'castrate two hundred pigs for Jeremiah
Johnston, at Tullywhisker, 10.00 am sharp' with some scribbled
direction for finding the farm - the message leapt off the page. My
heart was racing - a cold shiver ran down my spine. I suddenly
realised that I had never castrated a pig. At that stage of my career,
as a neophyte vet, the thought of castrating one pig was frightening
enough; the idea of castrating two hundred pigs beggared belief.
Mathematics was one of my few strong points. According to my
calculation, that meant that I had to remove surgically four hundred
testicles! I could hear Mr Billy MacCaskie's reassuring words ringing
in my ears; 'I'll have a good man waiting to help you.' Unfortunately,

the 'good man'- my mentor - would be engaged elsewhere, burying yet another farmer.

Having finished all the calls I retired to bed early, totally exhausted. I had survived my first day in veterinary practice. I could not sleep. I knew the telephone was just beside my bed. It might ring at any time. What nightmare calls awaited, I wondered, as I lay staring at the ceiling. I felt very lonely in my small bed in this little room - what a contrast from my room at Trinity. No friends to talk to. Complete silence, apart from the occasional sound of owls hooting in the oak tree outside my bedroom window. If I were to maintain my sanity, I knew instinctively that somehow I was going to have to adjust rapidly to this new way of life. Fortunately, I had brought my trusty wind-up alarm clock with me that had proved its worth all through my university days at Trinity. It was made in Germany and had PETER emblazoned on the clock face. I set "Peter" for an early start and placed it on the small bedside table so that I could go to sleep with confidence knowing that the banging of the hammer on the dual bells would awaken the dead. I finally drifted into the land of nod, wondering with apprehension how I would tackle Jeremiah Johnson and his two hundred pigs.

Every dog has his day
I was suddenly awakened by the persistent and incessant banging of my alarm clock. To my surprise, I had actually slept soundly - not a single telephone call had disturbed my slumbers. The sun was shining. After a quick breakfast, I set off in search of Tullywhisker. As I gingerly opened the five-barred gate that led to Tullywhisker, a faint glimmer of hope came into my mind. Perhaps half of the pigs would be gilts (or females) and would not need to be castrated. In the sunshine, after a good night's rest, things did not seem quite so bad after all.
Jeremiah Johnson was waiting by the piggery door. It was turning into a scorching hot day. The smell was already pretty bad. I knew that the summer sunshine and searing heat would accentuate the stench. Jeremiah Johnson was a small, stocky man, with short arms and legs, small hands and feet. He had a large prominent nose, rather pointed ears, and small, dark, slit-like eyes, set back in their sockets. He had thick, sandy-coloured hair, bushy eyebrows and a ruddy complexion. My first impression was that he had a somewhat porcine appearance himself. He was a laconic man. He did not utter a single word as he led the way into the dimly lit piggery.
Tullywhisker was a complete contrast to Tullymuck. It was a highly organised farm. There was a large expanse of concrete in the pristine yard. One got the impression that it was probably religiously hosed down with water every morning.
I could feel the sweat on my brow; the intense heat of the sun was absorbed by the low corrugated iron roof, just above my head. On viewing the assembled pigs, they were all totally relaxed, not moving, but keeping a beady eye on me with anticipation.

An Irish vet looks back
by Fergus Ferguson ©

Not a word was said as Jeremiah grabbed the first pig by its hocks and turned it upside down, grasping it with his knees, between his legs, in the traditional fashion. As I braced myself in readiness to make the first uncertain incision, scalpel and scalpel blade in hand, I could not help thinking about the perilously close proximity of the piglet's testicles to Jeremiah's groin. I hoped and prayed that the pig would stop wriggling. The peculiar part about this particular procedure was that Jeremiah was perfectly relaxed about everything. I suppose he had seen thousands of pigs castrated before and this occasion was no different from any previous veterinary encounter.
The relief was unbelievable when I completed my first pig castration. It took me all of fifteen minutes. The luck seemed to be running. The next three piglets that Jeremiah caught were gilts. My second castration lasted ten minutes and the third five minutes. What a pity Paddy was otherwise engaged. I could hear him say: 'You're on the pig's back now, Fergus!' I felt that he would have been proud of his most recent protégé as I castrated the last pig in thirty seconds flat.

Jeremiah had placed a couple of large metal buckets near to hand as receptacles for the innumerable testicles. When the job was finally finished, he lifted the buckets of testicles and carried them outside the piggery. Two large, hungry collie sheepdogs were eagerly rushing round in circles in the farmyard. It was obvious from their excited behaviour that they knew precisely what delicacies awaited them. Without further ado, Jeremiah threw the testicles one after the other into the air, for the dogs to catch. With one sudden gulp each testicle was ravenously devoured. I knew working collies had voracious appetites, but these two dogs, judging by their frenetic activity, looked as if they had not had a square meal for weeks. Finally they collapsed - bloated. They had had enough. Every dog has its day and this certainly was theirs.

Ixodes Ricinus - a fiendish little beast
On my third day at Tullymuck, I received a call to see a sick cow. Business was very quiet for Paddy, so he willingly said he would navigate. Apparently, Paddy had heard about this client, but they had not actually met. Paddy said he thought he owned just a few beef suckling cows and kept them at grass in a bog meadow by a lough. When we finally drew to a halt in the enclosed yard at the smallholding, the client emerged from one of the buildings. Before we had a chance to alight from the car, Mickey Muldoon, a well-known comedian and local character, put his foot on the running board of the car, poked his head in through the window and enquired: 'Who are you?'
'I'm the vet,' I replied. 'I've come to see your sick cow.'
Mickey, knowing that he was now centre stage, looked quizzically in Paddy's direction and enquired, 'And who's your man?'
'He's the undertaker,' I replied.
Aware of the incongruity of the situation, he said, with a wry smile, 'You're a fine pair of boys to come to visit my sick cow. I was counting on you curing her, not burying her.'

An Irish vet looks back
by Fergus Ferguson ©

Mickey led us across the yard. The Hereford cow was standing suckling her calf inside a lean-to shack. Restrained by a chain attached to a stout oak post, she was extremely depressed, constipated, breathing heavily and not chewing the cud. I could see by the hollow depression on her left flank that she had not eaten for several days. Her temperature was 107 degrees, and she was patently a very sick cow. Having carefully listened to her heart and lungs with my stethoscope, I was just on the point of diagnosing pneumonia, when Paddy whispered, 'Have you checked her water, Fergus?'

Paddy knew from his previous experience of this locality that it was a suitable habitat for the terrible tick, Ixodes Ricinus. This fearsome little creature lives on the grass and attaches itself to the body of grazing cattle as they pass. It then injects a parasite that invades the red blood corpuscles, causing haemolysis and a massive release of haemoglobin into the urine. This was the classical British Red Water Disease and is a serious and potentially fatal disease.

I was in Paddy's debt yet again. 'Have you seen her pass water, Mickey?' I enquired. Mickey looked perplexed but he replied that he hadn't. I will have to do a test to try to make your cow pass water. I tickled the cow's vulva, and then stretched the entrance to the bladder, with my fingers. I had never done this before but I'd seen the vets do this in Red Water areas when I was seeing practice. Consequently, I was rather apprehensive. I waited, and waited and waited. After what seemed to be an eternity but was probably only about two minutes, to my great relief, Mickey's cow squatted down and passed urine. It was the classical Port Wine colour. Mickey, looking aghast, exclaimed: 'Begorra, someone's been feeding her buckets of beetroot!' I assured Mickey that it really had nothing to do with beetroot but it was in fact Red Water fever. The appropriate injection was given to try to stop the parasite multiplying in Mickey's cow's red blood cells, together with instructions left to drench the cow with butter mixed with a solution of brown sugar, to alleviate her constipation. Once I knew what the correct diagnosis was, I explained to Mickey the way that the disease worked and said that any other cattle that might be grazing on the same pasture could be at risk of infection. I suggested to Mickey that if it were possible, he should bring them indoors but if this was not possible, they should be moved to pastures that were known not to harbour the dreaded little tick, Ixodes Ricinus.

What disasters would have happened to me and the animals under my care, had it not been for the indispensable help of my modest, but somewhat unorthodox, adviser, I wondered.

The MacAskie family eventually returned from the south of France and by the look of their sunburnt faces, the weather had been very kind to them. Billy drew a cheque in my favour and thanked me for looking after the practice in his absence. I shook Billy's hand enthusiastically and thanked him for the cheque. This cheque boosted my confidence considerably since it was the first payment that I had received as a fully-fledged practising veterinary surgeon. I then shook hands with Paddy and thanked him for all his invaluable help and guidance during my first locum in veterinary practice.

It was with a mixture of sadness and relief that I said goodbye to Tullymuck.

Ballybogillbo

News travels fast in the Irish countryside. A Mr Roderick Fitzherbert, a racing man, from Co Armagh, had heard on the grapevine that I was doing a locum at Tullymuck. He wondered if I would be willing to run his practice when Billy MacCaskie returned from holiday. It seemed that Mr Fitzherbert was of a nervous disposition with a pronounced stutter, so, as a matter of practicality, his charming wife spoke to me on the telephone.

'Roderick,' she said, 'will be flying around the countryside - the races at Goodwood, Haydock and Newbury. Don't worry, everyone will be here: Stuart the student, Mrs O'Shaughnessy the cook and Tommy the yardman. Of course, I'll be here myself. We'll all be backing you. When can you come?'

I had seen photographs of Mrs Fitzherbert in the Irish Tatler - captured at the races at Leopardstown and Punchestown. There was no denying it, Mrs Fitzherbert was stunningly attractive. An elegant woman, who usually had scores of admirers in close attendance, just like bees around the proverbial honey pot. Following all the excitement and exertions at Tullymuck, I had planned to have a holiday, but when I heard Mrs Fitzherbert's dulcet tones, I felt my resolve slipping; I knew that I would shortly be wending my way westward to work. My holiday would have to wait.

Since I had no car of my own, Mr Fitzherbert had arranged for his yardman, Tommy, to collect me, together with my belongings, and bring me to the practice. On the way from Tullymuck, Tommy, a most affable man, had talked non-stop about the Fitzherberts. I had learned that not only was Roderick Fitzherbert a vet, he was also well-known in the racing world. He owned a farm and thoroughbred stud, just outside Ballybogillbo. The stud had produced several very good racehorses and the yearlings sold well at the famous Houghton Sales at Newmarket. They also had several horses (both flat race and national hunt) in training at the Curragh, in County Kildare. Tommy worked part time at the stud and part time at the practice, and seemed to know everyone and everything there was to know about Ballybogillbo.

Following my escape from Tullymuck, it was mid-afternoon by the time we arrived at Ballybogillbo. As we drew up outside the elegant, typically Irish Georgian townhouse, I instinctively felt that life here in the centre of Ballybogillbo was indeed going to be a world apart from the cut and thrust of life at Tullymuck.

Tommy deposited me with my suitcases on the pavement in front of the house and went to garage the car. Drumlister House looked most welcoming: substantial, with sliding sash windows, three storeys under a Welsh slate roof, a solid front door complete with a traditional semicircular fan light above. A polished brass plate to the right of the front door read: <u>Roderick Fitzherbert M.R.C.V.S., Consultations by Appointment</u>. I climbed the short flight of stone steps that led to the front door and used the elegant brass knocker to announce my arrival. The brass handle turned slowly. A large lady with a welcoming smiling face opened the door. A primly starched apron covered her ample bosom. From Tommy's description, I realised this must be the unflappable Mrs O'Shaughnessy, the cook. Introductions over, she informed me that Mrs Fitzherbert was driving Mr Fitzherbert to the airport. When they had departed from Drumlister House there was no outstanding work - all was under control. However, in their absence, there had been a sudden and unexpected influx of calls.

'I'll show you to your room,' she said. 'When you are ready, come down to the kitchen and meet Stuart. He is waiting there for you.'

Once inside the front door I immediately noticed the ornate, winding staircase. Mrs O'Shaughnessy led the way up the stairs, giving me a brief introductory tour of the first floor - a series of beautifully proportioned, well-appointed rooms with high ceilings, all with open fireplaces: sitting room, dining room, drawing room and study. Antique furniture, together with expensive fabric, abounded. We continued up the winding staircase to the second floor, where she showed me to my cosy room, that appeared to have been a former nursery, and indicated that the bathroom was across the landing. There were great views over Ballybogillbo.

'Tea will be ready in five minutes in the kitchen,' she announced, and departed rapidly to answer the telephone, which sounded as if it were ringing somewhere in the basement. I had a feeling I was really going to enjoy living and working here.

Five minutes later, I was running down the stairs in search of tea - the sound of the telephone ringing again led me to the kitchen, which I discovered at the back of the house, near the surgery. With typical Irish casualness, notwithstanding the air of gentility, the hub of family life and the veterinary activities took place in the cellar - well, not exactly the cellar, more a split-level ground floor. Due to the lie of the land, one went down half a flight of stairs to the kitchen and surgery. A large range, polished with black lead faced me.

As I entered the room I heard Mrs O'Shaughnessy announcing to another client, in her customary phlegmatic fashion, as if she were totally accustomed to reassuring the entire county, that 'a grand man will be on his way shortly'. From the kitchen windows I could see a yard with outbuildings, garage and a walled garden. Stuart was seated at the huge kitchen table that was positively groaning under the weight of a traditional Irish high tea: a selection of neatly-cut sandwiches, plates of scones and cake. Mrs O'Shaughnessy introduced us and invited me to be seated and have something quickly, before setting off on our list of calls. I could see from the piece of paper which she was casually waving in the air that the list of calls was as long as her arm.

'Eat up, Fergus' said Mrs O'Shaughnessy, in a motherly fashion. 'You've got a long night ahead of you.'

I quickly swallowed some tea. 'Perhaps we should be on our way, Stuart. Which is the most urgent case?'

Mrs O'Shaughnessy nonchalantly mentioned that Jack Smith from Tullycranky had just returned from market to find a cow had unexpectedly calved and was stretched to look a tele-cry out on the ground. I could feel the colour draining from my face as panic set in. She had obviously read my thoughts.

An Irish vet looks back
by Fergus Ferguson ©

'Don't worry Fergus, Stuart knows all the farmers and the district. You won't have any trouble.'
Stuart and I jumped into the vet's car and sped off to find the recumbent cow at Tullycranky.
'I hope it's not milk fever, Stuart. If it is, I fear that after this length of time she may be dead.'
When we arrived at Tullycranky, the weather-beaten farmer greeted us with a woebegone expression and dejected demeanour.
'It's my best cow,' he announced. 'You're too late, she's dead!'
We followed him into a spacious stone loose box. The large Friesian cow was lying stretched out in a deep bed of straw. A hungry newborn calf with a wistful look in its eye, was standing beside her, lowing forlornly. The cow felt very cold and did not appear to be breathing. She had a huge udder that was running copious quantities of milk. I gently touched the cow's cornea and was relieved to notice she may have blinked. I did not think that Jack had noticed this, as he could not bear to watch us and as he was looking out over the half door of the loose box, staring blankly at the sky in a disconsolate fashion. When a vet finds himself in a situation like this, the art of veterinary medicine decrees that it is advantageous to persuade the owner to go away and do something useful.
'Fetch a bucket of warm water, soap and a towel, as quickly as possible, please.' I requested. 'I think there's a chance.'
Jack's mood suddenly improved and he headed off forthwith towards the farmhouse, obviously pleased to be involved and have something constructive to do. The cow was <u>in extremis</u> and very close to death from milk fever (low blood calcium). Prompt action was required if she were to be saved.
'Do you know where Mr Fitzherbert keeps his flutter valve and bottles of calcium, Stuart?' I enquired.
I knew that there was no time to wait for Jack and the warm water, which is sometimes used to heat the calcium solution on a cold day. As I anticipated, the cow did not move a muscle when I slipped the wide bore needle into her vein. I knew it would be a race against time. I kept my fingers crossed, hoping that the calcium would start to take effect before her heart stopped beating. When I had completed the first intravenous transfusion, the cow suddenly began to stir. I could just feel a very weak pulse. She then started to breathe slowly. Well done, old girl, I thought, as Stuart passed me the second bottle. I remembered the old saying - where there's life, there's hope - and prayed that it would apply in regard to Jack's cow.
Calcium borogluconate was a relatively new drug. Its dramatic effect was not yet widely known amongst the farming community. Hitherto, the cow's udder had to be inflated with air using a bicycle pump - a most unsatisfactory and dangerous state of affairs. When we had finished the intravenous transfusions, I asked Stuart to help me raise her head. I secured it with a rope halter and we managed to roll her on to her sternum. She was now breathing steadily and was looking for her calf. To our astonishment she suddenly staggered to her feet. I pulled on the shank of the rope halter to help steady her head. Out of the

corner of my eye, I could see Jack opening the farmhouse door. He walked briskly across the yard carrying the bucket of warm water, soap and towel. He stopped to open the half door of the loose box. As he glanced in, to his utter amazement, his favourite cow was standing contentedly suckling her calf.

'God bless us, save us and take care of us,' he exploded with relief. 'Yiz have brought her back from the dead!' His gnarled face was a mixture of bewilderment, relief and delight. I can hear him yet and see his face as if it were yesterday.

The news of this miraculous cure spread throughout the countryside like wildfire. This was wonderful in the short term but these miracles are a double-edged sword: they definitely cut both ways. Eventually, some farmers expect miracles to be performed as a matter of course.

We continued to wade through the ever-increasing list of calls. Mrs O'Shaughnessy kept dispatching further cases to us via the remarkably efficient local grapevine. Very few farmers possessed telephones in the mid sixties. Detours and stops were made at each local pub or post office, just in case a message may have been left for the peripatetic vet that, at this time of the year, inevitably seemed to be the case.

Will-o'-the-Wisp

It was long past midnight when we drove up the side of the mountain en route to the last call of the day at Josiah Judge's from Ballymacatoo. The night was clear and the moon was full. All the farmers had been busy making hay; most of it had been cut and turned. The weather was set fair; the hay would soon be ready for baling. It was just the type of evening where one might see Will-o'-the-wisp in a bog meadow. I knew the last call was a sow with farrowing fever. This is a septicaemia or fever that sometimes develops after farrowing. The mountain farm was as quiet as a graveyard. The ghostly white contours of a barn owl startled us as it flew silently out of the stone barn, just skimming over our heads. This gave Ballymacatoo and eerie atmosphere.

To my surprise, Stuart suddenly said, 'Mr Fitzherbert frequently throws small pebbles at the upstairs windows of farmhouses, if he cannot see any sign of life!'

I am a great believer in keeping to tradition, particularly when faced with an unusual or unorthodox situation. By the light of the moon, I gathered a few small, round pebbles from the pathway which led to the farmhouse door and threw them carefully, one at a time, at each upstairs window, pausing briefly on each occasion to see if someone drew back the curtains. Eventually, following several unsuccessful attempts, the outline of a lanky man in a state of undress, attired only in his ragged night-shirt, appeared at one of the windows. Sliding the bottom half of the sash upwards, he pushed his skeletal frame out of the open window.

On recognising the vet's motorcar in the moonlight, he declared, 'Ah sure you're a grand man, vet. I knew you wouldn't let me down. Just hold your horses and I'll be with you just as fast as my legs will carry me.'

An Irish vet looks back
by Fergus Ferguson ©

Minutes later Josiah appeared fully clothed and led the way into a small, low piggery, by the light of a hissing and glowing Tilley lamp. He was so intent on showing us the way to his sick sow, he didn't realise that his flies were undone. The sow was lying stretched out in a deep bed of fresh straw. As my eyes became accustomed to the dimly lit piggery, I could see that she was very depressed and breathing rapidly. Her udder was extremely swollen and painful to the touch. As I removed the thermometer from its case, I could barely read it by the scant light of the Tilley lamp. I grabbed the sow's curly tail in my left hand, raising it to enable me to insert the thermometer into her rectum. I then applied gentle sideways pressure to the thermometer to ensure that its bulb was in intimate contact with the rectal mucous membrane. Her temperature was 107 degrees. Clearly she was suffering from mastitis and might also have an infection in the womb (metritis). The twelve little piglets were very hungry and were all frantically trying to suckle from their mother's udder, but to no avail. I inserted my arm into the depths of the sow's uterus to make sure that she had finished farrowing. She had indeed. There were no retained piglets. It was indeed a severe case of farrowing fever. Penicillin and pituitary extract were injected deeply into the muscle of the sow's neck. The penicillin normally cures the mastitis and septicaemia. The pituitary extract evokes the 'let down' of milk. We waited to assess the response to it. Before you could say Jack Robinson, the sow's udder was pouring with milk and all the piglets were feeding contentedly. I reassured Josiah that, despite her collapsed state, his sow should make a good recovery, once the penicillin had had the opportunity to take effect, much to his relief.
As we drove down the mountain track from Ballymacatoo, I stopped the car at the next five-barred wooden field gate and turned off the engine. The night was still. Leaning on the top bar of the gate, we could smell the wonderful fragrant aroma of the new-mown hay. The ground underfoot was boggy. The awe-inspiring reflection of the full moon in the water of the lough just beyond the fields was quite magical. The dark outline of the next mountain range was just visible in the distance. All day in the small hay meadows, the corncrake had been uttering its loud, persistent, rasping song, 'crake, crake, crake', not unlike the continuous turning of a wooden rattle. Suddenly, I saw a ghostly pale-bluish flickering flame move silently across the meadow, causing the new-mown hay to dance spookily up and down. It was Will-o'-the-wisp. Having witnessed this with my own eyes for the first time, sent shivers down my spine. I now realised why so many stories of ghostly apparitions in the bog meadows were recounted around turf fires in the thatched cottages on cold winter's nights. The elderly Professor of Chemistry had explained the phenomenon to us at Trinity. This phosphorescent light, seen in the Irish bog meadows, was caused by the combustion of methane gas, also known as firedamp or marsh gas. Instinctively, I felt that tomorrow was going to be another torrid day - good news for the farmers.

'A handful of sand?'

After what seemed to be an extremely short night's sleep, I woke to
another scorching summer's day. The bed was extremely comfortable. It
would have been all too easy to turn over and return to the arms of
Morpheus. However, duty called. The aroma wafting up the stairs from
the kitchen made me hurry through the bathroom. On our way home in the
moonlight, Stuart had described Mrs O'Shaughnessy's breakfasts. I felt
I must not miss my first opportunity to sample one. If it only tasted
half as good as it smelt, I would be happy. I discovered that everyone
had breakfast together around the large kitchen table. I really was
looking forward to meeting the lady whose voice had persuaded me that
her husband's need of a locum was greater than my need of a holiday.
As I walked into the kitchen, Mrs Fitzherbert greeted me with a
disarming smile, introduced herself and welcomed me to Drumlister
House. She had a relaxed, confident manner - a lady with a certain <u>je
ne sais quoi</u>. She invited me to join the happy gathering at the
breakfast table and apologised for having been unable to welcome me.
'I had to take Mr Fitzherbert to the airport yesterday afternoon,'
explained Mrs Fitzherbert. 'As you know, he has gone to Goodwood. We
have been discussing "the form". You may have gathered, we are all
ardent racing enthusiasts. The main race today is the Sussex Stakes.
The going is good to firm, so there should be a large field. We have
all had a flutter.'
As she spoke, the telephone rang. It was Mr Fitzherbert calling from
his hotel. Apparently, as a matter of practicality, it had been agreed
some long time ago that Mrs O'Shaughnessy would place the bets on his
behalf. He was always in a tearing hurry. That fact, combined with his
speech impediment, often meant that his rather garbled instructions
were not always understood by the Bookmakers.
After giving his instructions for the bets, he enquired, 'How's Fergus
getting on? What calls have come in?'
'Jack Watt from Drumshambo has just called,' Mrs O'Shaughnessy replied.
'He has a "beast" with head blain and wants a visit urgently.'
On hearing about this emergency, Mr Fitzherbert became very agitated
and started stuttering down the telephone at an alarming rate.
'Tell Fergus to give the "beast" a handful of sand,' he said and
replaced the receiver.
On this particular morning, the telephone line had been very bad.
There was a large amount of background noise. Mr Fitzherbert's stammer
and general impatience exacerbated the situation. Mrs O'Shaughnessy
looked extremely perplexed.
'Fergus, as you may have gathered,' Mrs O'Shaughnessy dutifully
reported, 'Jack Watt telephoned just before you came downstairs this
morning. He has a "beast" with head blain. Mr Fitzherbert says to
tell you to give it a handful of sand!'
 'A handful of sand, Mrs O'Shaughnessy? Are you sure?'
Everyone could see that I was puzzled. Head blain in cattle is an
acute allergic disease, known as urticaria, when the subcutaneous
tissue of the head suddenly swells in a very dramatic fashion. This
'handful of sand' as a recommended treatment did not make sense to me.

An Irish vet looks back
by Fergus Ferguson ©

Mrs Fitzherbert, who was used to the infinite problems caused by her
husband's frequent stutterings, suddenly postulated, 'Do you think he
meant, "Give it Anthisan", Fergus?' Mrs Fitzherbert's feminine logic
had solved the mystery. She could see by my nodded approval that the
phonetic approach had worked- "a handful of sand" really did sound like
"Anthisan". Anthisan, an antihistamine injection, must certainly have
been exactly what Mr Fitzherbert meant, since it was the appropriate
treatment for this condition. Every time I see the drug Anthisan, it
still reminds me of Mr Fitzherbert and his "handful of sand"!
However, that was not the end of the matter. Mrs O'Shaughnessy had a
much bigger problem. Which horse to back on the 2.30 race at Goodwood,
Wanderlust or Prendergast? A quick look at The Sporting Life revealed
Prendergast to be the hot favourite at 2:1. However, there was an
outsider at 30:1, with a similar sounding name - Wanderlust. What were
we to do? There was no way of contacting Mr Fitzherbert, since he
would have left his hotel and would be well on his way to Goodwood by
now.
This farcical situation reminded me of the old army anecdote, whereby
the first soldier in the line of troops was given a message and was
asked to pass it on to the next man and so on down the line. The
initial message was "Send reinforcements we're going to advance".
However, by the time the message reached the end of the line, the last
soldier received a somewhat garbled version: "Send three and four pence
(three shillings and four pence) we're going to a dance!"
Mrs Fitzherbert decided that we should take a consensus of opinion.
She asserted that it must have been Wanderlust, since she felt that her
husband seldom backed a hot favourite. Tommy thought Mr Fitzherbert
might have planned to back the outsider Wanderlust on the course, in
the hope that the odds on the red hot favourite Prendergast might
lengthen by the time the word reached Ballybogillbo. That way he would
have been able to hedge his bets. Mrs O'Shaughnessy felt almost
certain that he had said Wanderlust, although she could not be sure,
because of his stutter and the bad line. Stuart thought that at such
very short odds as 2:1 on Prendergast, it was hardly worth placing a
bet.
'What do you think, Fergus?' Mrs Fitzherbert enquired.
'I don't really study "form",' I replied. 'I feel the quickest way to
ruin a man is fast women and slow horses.'
'I take it from your flippant remark that you have abstained, Fergus?'
Mrs Fitzherbert retorted.
I nodded.
'So far, we have three in favour of Wanderlust at 30:1 and one in
favour of Prendergast at 2:1. You have your answer Mrs O'Shaughnessy.
Ring the bet through to the bookmakers. Fergus, you and Stuart had
better be off to administer "the handful of sand",' she quipped with a
roguish smile. Perhaps my earlier remark had been forgiven.

A hair of the dog
As we returned that night, we learned that Mr Fitzherbert had been
given a hot tip, reputed to have come straight from the horse's mouth

that Prendergast would win. The horse had been well ahead of the field
until his saddle had slipped, one length short of the finishing post,
which had left the field clear for Wanderlust. By accident, we had
backed the wrong horse but had, in the event, picked the winner at
30:1!
I had been at Drumlister House for almost a week when Mrs Fitzherbert
suddenly announced over breakfast, 'It's your night off tonight,
Fergus. Apart from days away at the races, Mr Fitzherbert has one
night off a week - every Saturday night. The other vet in the town
Mickey Hickey, covers the practice for him. I've booked a table for
three at the local hotel. Stuart will come as well. There's plenty of
money in the kitty following the unexpected win with Wanderlust at
Goodwood. You both deserve a good night out after all your hard work
this week.'
When we arrived at the Tipperary Arms, I could see that Mrs Fitzherbert
was on cloud nine and absolutely in her element. There was a general
buzz in the atmosphere. The hotel was full of racing people who had
all heard about the surprise windfall. Mrs Fitzherbert, always a very
generous lady, slipped the barman a ten-pound note and told him to pour
everyone a large drink.
After a really good meal, several stiff drinks pressed on me by Mrs
Fitzherbert, my head was beginning to swim.
'Have one for the road, Fergus. There's no need to worry, Stuart is
driving us home.'
Shortly, a rather large Irish whiskey was gently pushed across the
table in my direction. Just as "last orders" were being called, Mrs
Fitzherbert was summoned to the hotel telephone.
'I'm afraid you will have to go straight away on an urgent call,
Fergus,' she declared on her return. 'I know it's your night off, but
Mickey Hickey's motor car has ended up in a sheugh and they can't pull
him out. I suggested to Mickey that he might like to travel by
Shanks's mare but he said it's too far to walk. A cow's down and flat
out with milk fever. She'll be dead if you don't attend soon. Stuart
will drive. Drop me off at Drumlister House and go as quickly as you
can. It's Archie O'Toole from Derrygoon.'
As soon as the balmy night air hit me, I knew that I should not have
accepted the last double whiskey from Mrs Fitzherbert. My head was
spinning and I could hardly see my nose in front of my face. I felt as
if I was walking in fog. Stuart, fortunately, had had very little to
drink and knew the way to Derrygoon. It was a very dark night. As we
drove into the isolated farmyard, I could see a paraffin lamp (the only
source of light) flickering in the breeze, just inside the stone shed.
'I'm in here,' called a voice. It was Archie O'Toole, holding the
lamp.
As I groped my way into the barn, I tripped over the recumbent cow. I
had not noticed her in the darkness. She had recently calved, was flat
out with milk fever and close to death. Archie had been away all day
helping his neighbour make hay; he had totally forgotten that his cow
was due to calve. As I lay on the straw bed beside the cow, the entire
loose-box was going round and round. I could barely stand up.

An Irish vet looks back
by Fergus Ferguson ©

With slurred speech I instructed Stuart to bring the Calcium Borogluconate, the flutter valve, the wide bore needle and a strong torch. With more luck than judgement, I managed to push the needle into the vein.

'Now get two bottles of calcium into her, Stuart, as quick as you can.' As soon as the second bottle of calcium disappeared into the vein, the cow suddenly started to recover. As she staggered to her feet, I realised that I would have to move away from the cow fairly quickly, to avoid being trampled underfoot. I crawled across the straw and sat in the corner of the shed. The cow was now safely on her feet with her calf contentedly suckling from her udder.

In Ireland, in the mid- sixties, strange to relate, clients did not seem to mind if the vet was blind drunk. So long as he actually attended and the animal recovered, no one appeared to be the slightest bit concerned. There was so much work to be done and not enough vets to do it. A vet who had had "one over the eight" was definitely better than no vet at all.

The following morning, Mrs O'Shaughnessy had cooked everyone the usual substantial breakfast: bacon, eggs, sausages, tomato, mushrooms and black pudding. Mrs Fitzherbert was as bright as a button and her normal effervescent self.

'And how did you fare with Archie O'Toole's cow at Derrygoon, Fergus?' she enquired. 'Did you arrive in time?'

'Yes, we did and she's fine.' I mumbled.

'How are you feeling, Fergus?' she teased.

'I feel as if I have tripped over a straw and a hen has kicked me!' I retorted.

'I won't offer you a hair of the dog that bit you. Mrs O'Shaughnessy has a long list of calls, so you and Stuart had better be on your way.' Fortunately for me, Stuart, who was the soul of discretion, kept his counsel about my having directed proceedings from a prostrate position in the straw.

My locum days in Ireland continued in a totally laissez-faire fashion. All the vets knew each other. I was passed on, as it were, from practice to practice. I did not mind in the least. It was all grist to the mill. As far as I was concerned, the more experience I could obtain in different localities, the better. It was a wonderful opportunity to meet different types of people and see the countryside. However, I was beginning to feel the strain of sole responsibility of running single-handed practices. I was also mindful that I needed to address my career prospects: a rolling stone gathers no moss. Perhaps it was time for me to settle down.

In those days in Ireland, everything was happy-go-lucky and informal: no interviews, trial periods, introductions or other niceties. As a matter of course, I was thrown in at the deep end and had to fend for myself. This devil-may-care approach to life suited not only the vets but the clients as well. Everything is completely different now: written advertisements and mandatory replies, interviews, written references, probationary periods, careful supervision, colleagues available for consultation and second opinions, assistance with

An Irish vet looks back
by Fergus Ferguson ©

anaesthetics and surgery. In the early days, I always seemed to be
hanging on by the skin of my teeth: wonderful for the initiative but
bad for the nervous system. _In extremis_, God helps those who help
themselves or, in my case, the Devil looks after his own.

Bodmin Moor

After three months of being shunted from pillar to post around the countryside, in a type of veterinary pass-the-parcel, I decided it was time for me to take the initiative. Forthwith, an advertisement was placed in the mouthpiece of the veterinary profession, The Veterinary Record: "Recent graduate from Trinity College Dublin immediately available - anything considered. Box No..." I was inundated with replies - in excess of sixty letters were forwarded to me in the first week. One poor vet, practising on the Island of Rum, off the west coast of Scotland, had a three-year backlog of dehorning and castrating. Another vet had not had a holiday for ten years. I had spent some time seeing practice as a student in England and quite liked the way of life. One reply caught my eye. A four-man practice in the small market town of Roscorla, on the edge of Bodmin Moor in Cornwall, required an assistant. Following an initial telephone call, I packed my bags and boarded the night ferry from Belfast to Liverpool. I spent a sleepless night as the boat tossed and turned whilst it crossed the Irish Sea. The following morning I caught the connecting train to London. After a short journey on the Underground, I boarded the train at Paddington on the last leg of my journey. Feeling somewhat hungry by this time, I wandered along to the buffet car, where I was befriended by a man travelling to Penzance. He was a real character. We talked about everything under the sun, liberally washed down with pints of Guinness. The company was good and I did not count how many drinks we had had. The next thing I knew, the train was pulling in to Bodmin Road Station - a little halt in the middle of nowhere on Bodmin Moor. It was past midnight when I alighted from the train. Gas lamps dimly lighted the platform. The swirling autumn fog made visibility poor, giving the moorland station an eerie atmosphere of a horror-movie film set. As the train pulled out of the station, I realised that I was somewhat unsteady on my legs. Apart from the stationmaster, I was the only person on the platform. It seemed like the back of beyond.
True to his word, the senior partner was there to meet me. He was a well-built, good-looking man with a thick moustache, and in some ways he reminded me of the film star Clarke Gable. Very well-known in the

profession due to his involvement in veterinary politics, he talked
non-stop about his favourite subject all the way to his home in
Roscorla. At that stage of my career that was the last thing I had on
my mind. It was obvious to me that he was passionately interested in
all the controversial veterinary affairs that prevailed at that time.
Through the alcoholic haze, it seemed hopeful that we could develop a
rapport. As we crossed the Moor, he explained that he had an
arrangement with the local hotel in Roscorla. To enable the assistant
to attend to his veterinary duties, they provided full board and
lodging facilities. It was much too late to trouble the hotel, so he
had arranged that I should stay with him at his home at the surgery on
my first evening. When we arrived at Carn Vean, he invited me to join
him for a nightcap after my long journey. In reality, I was three
sheets to the wind already but whether he was aware of this or not, I
had no idea. Having put the world to rights, well into the small
hours, he showed me the way up the narrow creaking staircase to my
room. The next thing I knew, the maid was knocking on the door
bringing me a cup of early morning tea.

The Cornish Affirmative

My first job in the practice was to dehorn a herd of highland cows.
The farm was high above the Jamaica Inn, up a rough track, on the only
mountain in Cornwall - Brown Willy. The three Nancekevil brothers
lived on this isolated hill farm above Bolventor, called Upper
Trewartha. I announced to the first Mr Nancekevil that I was the new
vet. He replied, 'Oooffft'. (This was a type of sucking noise similar
to the sound one instinctively makes, caused by the rapid intake of
breath, when fingers are inadvertently trapped by a closing door.)
I said to the second Mr Nancekevil that I had come to dehorn the cows
and he also replied, 'Oooffft'.
I then turned to the third Mr Nancekevil and asked, 'Shall we start
with this cow?'
He also replied, 'Oooffft'.
By this time I was convinced that they were all afflicted by some
peculiar Cornish speech defect, probably as a consequence of years of
inbreeding in the isolation of the Moor.
Once I had anaesthetised all the cows' horns with local anaesthetic,
blocking the cornual nerves, I started to remove each horn one by one.
The horns were amputated using a length of cheese wire stretched
between two wooden handles, in a to-and-fro sawing action. The
friction created by the cheese wire produced a considerable degree of
heat, which tended to seal the blood vessels, thus minimising
haemorrhage. By the time we had finished there was a huge pile of
discarded horns lying on the ground beside the cattle crush.
The horns were magnificent specimens, each one about two feet long,
curving to a sharp point. These hairy moorland cattle seemed to thrive
well on Bodmin Moor, protected by their shaggy coats from the ravages
of the westerly wind and rain. I had planned to fly back to Ireland
for Christmas or the New Year, depending on the duty rosters, and asked
the brothers would they mind if I took some of the horns with me.

An Irish vet looks back
by Fergus Ferguson ©

They all replied enthusiastically with a collective, 'Oooffft'. They seemed genuinely pleased to be able to help me. It was then fashionable to mount such specimens and place them above the mantelpiece. I thought that perhaps my Mother might like to give them to her friends. The brothers, with obvious glee, filled a couple of hessian sacks with horns and loaded them into the back of my Morris Minor 1000 traveller motor car. This was the veterinary assistant's motorcar that was extremely useful for collecting dead animals which was the assistant's lot. Just before I left upper Trewartha, one of the Nancekivell brothers declared, "Proper job."

Occasionally, when all the calls were finished, the vets (three partners and the assistant) often met for a drink in the evening in the local pub. The purpose of this informal gathering was twofold. Ostensibly, it was to discuss the work in hand. In reality, it was to enjoy a relaxing drink with colleagues, exchange stories and develop an esprit de corps. I, of course, being the assistant, was "the boy". That was why the three partners had been saving all the jobs suitable for the fit, strong young vet, like dehorning a herd of Highland cows.

'How did you get on with the three Nancekevil brothers at Upper Trewartha?' asked the senior partner.

'Fine,' I replied, 'but they seem to have some peculiar speech impediment.'

Upon hearing my observation, they looked bewildered and another partner enquired, 'How did this apparent speech impediment manifest itself?'

I replied, 'Every time I asked them a question they replied with an "oooffft", sucking type noise.'

One of the partners, suddenly realising what the problem was, exclaimed, 'Ah sure 'tis the Cornish affirmative. All the moorland farmers use it. We forgot to tell you about it before you went up there.'

'Did you manage to remove all the horns?' the senior partner enquired anxiously. His worried expression rapidly turned to one of relief, when I replied in the affirmative.

The vernacular

One of the most important things for the vet to learn was the local farming vernacular. One did not learn this at college. Each area has its own particular phraseology and descriptive terms for certain conditions. The vet has to learn these as quickly as possible. The moorland farmers called all animals "her" irrespective of gender. The only exception to this rule was the "tom" cat, which, for some peculiar reason, was always described as him. A tom cat, of course, is an uncastrated male cat. There were other oddities. Nearly all sentences ended in "you". Verbs were frequently qualified by the use of the word "proper". "Maze" or "mazed" meant mad. For instance, if a bull was very nervous, temperamental or aggressive, the farmer might say to the vet, 'her's proper mazed, you!'

If the animal was uncooperative, awkward or contrary, the farmer would say, 'her's a proper old vule, you!' The moorland 'vule' seems to be Cornish for fool. All beef animals (including cows) are referred to as bullocks. So a herd of South Devon store cattle would be referred to (irrespective of gender) as a herd of bullocks.

Least said, soonest mended

The main road running across the moor - the A30 - was not like it is now. It was unfenced. Cattle wandered all over the Moor. If one drove along the A30 on a foggy November evening, the mist would descend over the Moor, enveloping everything in a thick shroud. Suddenly the motorist could be confronted with a creature standing in the middle of the road which looked like the Devil himself - a hairy face with two shining eyes, two huge horns and smoke coming out of its nose.

Most of my work was with sheep and cattle on Bodmin Moor. The Moor was a fascinating place in those days. It had been popularised by Daphne du Maurier in her famous book about smuggling and wrecking - Jamaica Inn. The true moorland farmers were wonderful people, once one got to know them. Anyone who came from east of the river Tamar was regarded as a foreigner. The farmers assumed that I must be English, since they would say, 'You must be one of they men who has come down from upwards!' ie east of the river Tamar, which divides the County of Cornwall from the rest of England. Initially they would treat me with indifference. However, when they realised that I was Irish, I was accepted - a fellow Celt. The real moorland farmer is very dark and swarthy - a race apart, and are said to be descendants of the shipwrecked sailors from the doomed Spanish Armada. I think it would probably be fairer to say that many of them came to Cornwall by sea from distant shores drawn by the mining - copper, lead and tin - in the 17th, 18th and 19th centuries. Tin mines in particular were scattered all over the county. There seemed to be a major influx of Welsh people who already possessed specialist mining skills.

The local hotel in Roscorla was very comfortable, the atmosphere was relaxed and friendly, and the food was excellent. Generally, the arrangement worked very well, since the young vet had plenty of company. However, occasionally, technical difficulties arose. Autumn calving was in full swing. As was the assistant's lot, I had been doing a series of morning visits. Almost every case seemed to be the removal of a cow's afterbirth - the large thick membrane which surrounds the calf whilst it is inside the cow's uterus. Normally, when the cow calves, the afterbirth is passed when the calf is born. Sometimes it is retained. Farmers were instructed to leave the afterbirth alone. If it was still attached on the fifth day after calving, the veterinary surgeon should be summoned, to remove it manually. After five days, the decomposing mass of tissue becomes extremely putrid and smelly. No matter how careful the vet was with washing and cleaning himself, the dreadful stench seemed to cling to him.

Arriving back at the hotel for lunch, the dining room was full of people. The waitress showed me to the only vacant seat at a table already occupied by three impeccably dressed elderly ladies. This chair was just beside the radiator. The central heating was set at maximum. The awful stench rapidly began to permeate the air of the entire dining room. There had been insufficient time for me to bathe or shower. The ladies suddenly became very uncomfortable as a result of the appalling smell. Their noses started to twitch. I could see from their repeated sniffing and distorted facial expressions that they were attempting to ascertain the source of the unpleasant odour wafting in their direction. Knowing glances were exchanged. I was acutely aware that I was the culprit. One of the ladies enquired of the young waitress (a farmer's daughter) if she knew what was causing the dreadful smell. The waitress gave me a knowing smile as she passed me my coffee.

'As soon as I drink this cup of coffee, I will be off on my afternoon visits. I think you will find that the problem will disappear!' I said.

This was the type of situation where "least said, soonest mended." Any description or attempted explanation of the actuality of the circumstances might only have exacerbated an already delicate situation, since the ladies were just about to embark upon their pudding.

Checkmate

In stark contrast to the hectic University social life at Trinity, it can be quite lonely for a young vet in a sparsely populated rural part of the English countryside. I had the good fortune to meet a young lady called Kate, who worked at the local bank as a teller. I had a few cheques to lodge so I thought I would visit the bank. A very attractive young lady was behind the counter. This was Kate. 'I am the new vet in Roscorla and I have a few cheques to lodge. My name is Fergus Ferguson. Can you help me, please?' Kate was extremely polite, vivacious and very efficient, attending to everything in a professional fashion. There seemed to be an immediate frisson between us. There were two young lady tellers working in the bank. Hitherto, on my visits, my business requirements had been attended to by Kate's colleague, a young married woman. Kate confessed to me later that the two cashiers had had an agreement that if I entered the bank in the future (if circumstances merited it), the two young ladies would go through the separate rear doors in a timely manner, Kate reappearing magically through the adjacent door to attend to my banking requirements.

A short time later, on my return to the surgery following a busy day amongst the farm animals on Bodmin Moor, the partners informed me that a young lady called Kate was bringing "Pluto", the family Alsatian dog to the surgery and had asked if I would be available to attend to the consultation. I donned a white consulting room coat, placing my stethoscope in my pocket in an attempt to look as professional as possible and hoped that I did not pong too much as a consequence of the innumerable consultations on the Moor. 'Hello Kate, I see from the practice records that this must be Pluto. What can I do to help you and Pluto?' Kate replied with a beguiling twinkle in her eye saying, 'I would like you to clip his toenails, please.' Pluto doesn't like having his toenails clipped so I am pleased to see you, Fergus.' I reacted with a degree of trepidation, 'I will try to make friends with him first and that might make him less nervous. By the way, does he like biscuits?' Kate nodded in approval so I produced some from my coat pocket inviting Pluto to smell them. He definitely liked biscuits and scoffed the lot. 'That seemed to work well, Fergus, since he seems to be less frightened already.' Animals live in a world of smells as I permitted Pluto to sniff around my brogue shoes. 'It is never easy clipping a large dog's toenails but the most important thing is to avoid going too close to sensitive parts of their toes.' I replied, in an attempt to reassure Kate. In the event, I managed to complete the exercise without much fuss. 'That seemed to work very well, Fergus. I can see that Pluto seems to like you and you didn't have to muzzle him.' Before we came to Cornwall the vets in Hampshire always insisted on placing a muzzle on Pluto's nose and this made Pluto very frightened when having his nails clipped. Following this professional praise, I tendered another biscuit and tickled Pluto under his chin.

'Fergus, I am having my twenty first birthday party in just over two weeks. It's at the Poldark hotel near the Bedruthan steps, just beyond Newquay. Would you like to come? All my friends will be there. I shall ask Mummy and Daddy to send you an invitation.' said Kate, with enthusiasm. 'Thank you for inviting me, Kate. I would be delighted to attend providing it does not clash with the duty rota. If you like, I can go through to the office to see if I am free.' Kate nodded, with anticipation. The luck seemed to be running. I discovered with delight that I was not on duty on the night in question. In due course, I received a formal invitation that was customary in the mid-60s. Perhaps my social life in Roscorla was taking a turn for the better.

It was a formal "black tie" evening, all the young ladies were wearing long colourful, chic ball gowns. On arrival, the band was playing and the party was in full swing. Kate was an outstanding dancer and moved to the music in an elegant and rhythmical style. Kate was wearing a fashionable full-length Jersey red dress, together with mermaid shoulder straps. This outfit complemented her long, flowing jet-black tresses to perfection. Kate was very definitely a woman in her prime. Introductions were made to her family and her large circle of friends which made me feel very much at home. Kate was very much in demand and all the young men surrounded her like bees round a honeypot. I could see that if I were to have an opportunity to win her affections, I would have to make a request for the pleasure of the next dance. Following a delicious supper, the dancing continued until the small hours. Even though the party was held on the north coast of rural Cornwall, it was a traditional but quintessentially English occasion. When an opportunity arose, I asked Kate if I could have the pleasure of the next dance. Fortunately it was a slow waltz. Eventually, I plucked up courage and asked Kate if she would like to join me for a drink at the local Bedruthan Steps hotel. To my great relief and joy, Kate replied in the affirmative. This was the start of an enchanting romance with Kate and Cornwall.

We shared many common interests, including our love of country life. On my weekends off duty, Kate would show me the delights of the Cornish countryside. The north Cornwall coast in particular is rugged and beautiful. The huge waves come straight in from America. Kate knew the area very well and in particular the most beautiful coastal walks.

An Irish vet looks back
by Fergus Ferguson ©

In the long dark winter evenings, we played chess. We particularly
liked the romantic atmosphere of the Jamaica Inn near Bolventor and
frequently played chess beside a huge roaring fire. The vets visited
the Jamaica Inn from time to time since there were a few farm animals
behind the Inn so the Innkeeper knew who I was. When I was on duty, I
frequently visited Kate's home. If there were any emergency calls, the
senior partner would telephone me there. Provided it was not too late,
Kate would accompany me. Kate's father was a popular and respected
businessman in Roscorla. The vets knew him well. One night, about
2.00 am, the practice received an emergency call. The senior partner,
thinking that I was on duty, tried to contact me at the hotel. There
was no answer. Unbeknown to him, I had changed duties with the other
partner to enable him to attend a social function the previous evening.
On that particular night, I was out with Kate. Receiving no response,
the senior partner assumed (wrongly) that I must be at Kate's home, so
he telephoned there. Apparently, for five long minutes, the air was
blue. Kate's father did not appreciate being disturbed from his
slumbers in the early hours. Being a light sleeper, the unexpected
telephone call had disturbed his sleep for the rest of the night.
Following the 2.00am contretemps, the dust finally settled and
fortunately the chess games continued. As a matter of course, I always
won. I was much more experienced at playing the game than Kate, so
this was not surprising. A few months later, there was a lull in the
proceedings and we did not play for some time. Out of the blue, Kate
suddenly challenged me, in her impish manner, to another game. It was
not long before I realised that I was in a jam. Checkmate soon
followed and Kate won the game. Kate then confessed that she had
borrowed a book on chess from the library and had been secretly
studying the game. After this admission, the tussles became much more
exciting, since we were now more or less evenly matched.

Evening Surgery

A short time after I arrived in Roscorla, the local doctor purchased
the premises next door to the veterinary surgery. The entrances to the
two properties were very similar. After a few minor modifications, the
doctor fixed his brass plate to the wall of his newly acquired
property, just beside the entrance door, and commenced practice. As a
rule, there were very few small animals to see at evening surgery.
Clients came with their animals to the waiting room, took a seat and
were seen on a first come first served basis. Shortly after the doctor
started practising next door, it was my turn to do evening surgery. On
returning from a busy day on the Moor, the waiting room was packed with
people and their animals. I quickly viewed the numerous assembled
clients and animals and prepared myself for an especially busy surgery.
I donned the traditional white coat, put my stethoscope in the pocket
and announced, 'First please.'

As I attended to the seemingly never-ending list of clients and their
animals, I noticed that an elderly lady had arrived and was sitting
quietly on her own in the corner of the waiting room. Dressed in a
full-length Harris Tweed coat, thick stockings and sensible brown
shoes, matching handbag and gloves, she had a small hat clamped firmly

An Irish vet looks back
by Fergus Ferguson ©

on her head, over her neat grey curls. Draped around her neck, tucked
inside her coat, was a contrasting silken scarf. The lady appeared to
be watching everyone nervously through her neat, black-rimmed
spectacles and did not have an animal with her. This was not
particularly unusual, since some people just came for advice.
When her turn finally arrived, I could see that she looked quite
worried as I said, 'Next please'. I escorted her into the consulting
room. It was a plain, high-ceilinged, old-fashioned room with a table,
a few chairs, sink, bookshelf and a glass-fronted cabinet, which held a
variety of instruments. I tried to put the lady at her ease, by
offering her a seat and enquiring how I could help.
With no hesitation whatever, she said, 'Doctor, I've had this dreadful
pain in my left side for the last week and its definitely getting
worse,' as she unbuttoned her coat. My mind was working overtime, she
was on the point of pulling up her jumper to show me exactly where the
pain was situated. I could see that from this lady's perspective,
nothing was amiss. The doctor had moved his premises to the other side
of town. The two surgeries had a very similar external appearance.
Both displaying the traditional shining brass plate beside the door and
boasting an entrance hall and waiting room inside. A man dressed in a
white coat with a stethoscope in his pocket appeared from time to time
saying, 'Next please'. Clients came and went. In her distressed
state, she had been completely oblivious to the fact that all the other
people who entered and left the consulting room were accompanied by
animals. I shall never forget her look of utter disbelief and horror,
when I hurriedly stopped her disrobing and gently informed her that
unfortunately I would be unable to assist, since I was a veterinary
surgeon, not a doctor.

The Moors' Murders

My arrival in the small market town of Roscorla coincided with the
dreadful tragedy that occurred on the other moors in the Midlands,
which became known nationally and internationally as the Moor's
Murders. The daily papers were full of it. The news seemed to worsen
day by day. Everyone was talking about the dreadful killings and the
searches for the missing children on the Moor.
During this time, I was busily catching up on the large backlog of
dehorning of cows. It was quite a gory job, since, from time to time
the arteries spurted blood, until the vet controlled the haemorrhage.
There were no facilities for washing clothes in the hotel. Each week I
brought my bloodstained clothing to the local cleaners. This shop was
run by two sisters - both upright, elderly spinsters. They did not
know me or what I did for a living. After a while, they started to
give me really strange looks, but did not ask any questions. They
appeared to be really frightened. Walking away from their shop, I
glanced over my shoulder and saw both sisters standing outside,
watching me intently. Suddenly, it dawned on me what might be on their
minds. Yes, I did things right out in the middle of the Moor and
always arrived back covered in blood. However, I do not think it was
the type of activity which they had in mind. I thought that perhaps I
owed them an explanation, to reassure them and allay any possible

fears. I returned to the shop and, without further ado, I explained to the frightened sisters, 'Perhaps I should have introduced myself, when I first came to your shop. I'm the new vet here in Roscorla. My name is Fergus Ferguson. I expect you know all the other vets at Carn Vean. They have been so busy that they are rather behind with the task of dehorning the cows out on the Moor. It has been saved up for my arrival - traditionally this is the assistant's job. I am sorry that there has been so much blood on my clothes. I'm afraid it's rather an occupational hazard. I hope it hasn't been too much of a problem for you and that you will continue to wash my clothes for me.'

The expression on the two ladies' faces changed dramatically as I disclosed the reality of my position. Firstly, they looked at me in fear. Then their expressions changed to incredulity and disbelief. Next they looked at each other. Finally, their expressions changed to relief. Neither of them knew what to say. I gave them both a reassuring smile and said I would return next week to collect my clean laundry.

Christmas Day

Being the boy, with no wife and children, the partners asked me would I be willing to be on duty on Christmas Day. This was my first Christmas in veterinary practice and I did not mind in the least.

The hotel maid woke me with the usual early morning cup of tea and a cheerful, 'Happy Christmas'. I staggered out of bed, stumbled across the room and drew back the curtains. To my surprise and delight, Roscorla, nestling beneath the hotel, had been transformed overnight by a thick blanket of snow - a picture postcard white Christmas.

Since it was freezing cold and the Moor was covered in a deep layer of snow, only dire emergencies were being dealt with. Halfway through the morning a cow collapsed with milk fever. It was a long way out on the Moor, half way between the Bronze Age stone circles known as the Hurlers and the Neolithic dolmen, Trethevy Quoit. The driving conditions were atrocious. One mile short of the farm, the road was blocked by a huge snowdrift. It was impossible to proceed any further by car. There was only one thing for it - I would have to travel the rest of the way on foot. Needs must when the Devil drives. As I quickly bundled all the necessary drugs and equipment into my bag, to my alarm I noticed that the calcium solution inside the bottles was frozen solid. I pulled on my wellington boots, smock coat and cap, and briskly sallied forth on foot through the snow. The wooden five-barred entrance gate to the farm was obstructed by a solid drift of snow. I clambered over the slippery, icy bars of the gate, carefully manoeuvring my bag and its contents, hoping that the glass bottles would not break.

Jonas Pengelly rushed out of the farmhouse to greet me. 'Thank goodness you've made it. Her's flat out on the straw and barely breathing, you!' The anxious young farmer led me directly to his cow. He had a herd of south Devon cows. I had visited the farm previously on several occasions for milk fever and calving cases. Fortunately he knew exactly what would be required and had a large galvanised metal bucket half full of warm water ready. I carefully placed two bottles

37

An Irish vet looks back
by Fergus Ferguson ©

of frozen calcium solution in the water. As soon as the solution had melted, I administered it intravenously as quickly as possible via a flutter valve. Amazingly, after a short while, the cow stood up and all was well. Jonas was extremely grateful. Thanking me profusely, he said, 'Come indoors and have a Christmas drink.'
It was much warmer inside the farmhouse kitchen. I was invited me to take a seat by the range and thaw out while he poured me a stiff drink. His wife, Janna, was sitting on a chair beside the farmhouse table. She had recently given birth. I could see that she was unwell and that Jonas was concerned about her. I had known them both for sometime, frequently having visited them for emergencies in all hours of the night. Jonas suddenly asked me if I would have a look at his wife who, by this time, was showing obvious signs of discomfort. Janna nodded in agreement. I enquired as to the nature of the problem and Jonas informed me that Janna was in considerable pain from mastitis. Both of them were adopting a totally matter of fact stance and it seemed clear that they were expecting me to pass a professional opinion. The strange thing about it was that neither of them showed the slightest bit of embarrassment. I explained to them that I was a veterinary surgeon and not a doctor. Consequently, I could not help them. Jonas, who was obviously very worried about Janna, then tried to persuade me to carry out the examination, saying, 'I have seen you do exactly the same thing on many occasions when the cows have had mastitis. We trust you and we know that you will do the right thing.' I reiterated that I could not help, emphasising that they must call the doctor. Jonas replied, 'I have already telephoned him, he won't come out. It's Christmas Day and the weather's too severe.'
'If the doctor cannot come out here to you, you must take Janna and the baby to visit him. Go and start up the Land rover. By the time Janna has swaddled the baby, the Land rover should be nice and warm.'
'Anything to declare, Sir?'
Having worked over the Christmas holiday, I was given a few days off for the New Year, so I could visit my family in Ireland. Having transferred the handsome Highland cattle horns from the hessian sacks to various holdall cases, I caught the aeroplane from Exeter to Dublin. Dublin Airport was then very small and low-key. While waiting for my turn to have my bags cleared by Customs, I spotted a Department of Agriculture notice: "Animal by-products - Foot and Mouth Disease, Anthrax - Regulations". Shock, horror. What had I done? Me, of all people. A practising veterinary surgeon. How stupid could one get, I asked myself. I thought that I had better come clean.
I told the official behind the desk that I had something to declare, pointing to the notice behind his head. After some brief questions, he looked around furtively to see if anyone was watching, before he hurriedly ushered me together with my trolley laden with the bulging bags, out through the back of the building and round to a little hut. Opening the door, I was shown a seat. 'Wait there. I'll see if Mr O'Brien is available.' Knocking on the inner office door and, without waiting for a reply, he opened it. I could see them whispering intently to each other. Mr O'Brien fumbled in his desk drawer and

eventually produced what looked like an official book of regulations.
Glancing in my direction from time to time, as he thumbed through the
pages of the circular. As they looked at me suspiciously, I
increasingly began to feel like a pariah.
Years of training had conditioned Mr O'Brien and his colleague to watch
out for people like me. I was shown into the smoke-filled room. The
desk was piled high with official-looking papers. The ashtray was
overflowing with stubbed cigarette butts. Perhaps I had stolen their
thunder by drawing their attention to the animal by-products and
confessing to them what was in my bags. You could hear the cogs
ticking. Judging by the puzzled look on their faces, I did not think
they had ever come across anything like this before. I thought that it
would only be fair to put them out of their misery.
'I am Fergus Ferguson, a veterinary surgeon. I have stupidly brought
these horns from Bodmin Moor in Cornwall as a gift for my mother in
North of Ireland. I forgot that Dublin, being in the Republic of
Ireland, is a separate jurisdiction from the United Kingdom. You had
better contact the Department of Agriculture about it. They will
probably confiscate them.'
The telephone call was duly made. The peculiar thing about Civil
Servants, in a situation like this, was that no one wanted to make a
decision. Having been passed from one department to another, finally
the Divisional Veterinary Officer, after in depth questioning about the
exact health status of the herd on Bodmin Moor, with the greatest
reluctance, seized the horns. The DVO was very polite and most
apologetic about it all and hoped that my mother would not be too
disappointed. It was explained that they would be treated chemically
and rendered sterile. This procedure would take about 6 weeks, after
which they would be available for collection.
'I will be back at work in Bodmin by then,' I explained.
'Never mind. Just drop in any time when you're passing through,' he
suggested, helpfully.
I expect that the horns are still awaiting collection, gathering dust
in the vaults of the Department of Agriculture!
When I was at home for the New Year, my parents mentioned that a
veterinary surgeon acquaintance was due to retire shortly and had been
in touch since he was looking for someone to take over his practice and
wondered whether I would be interested. Never wishing to refuse an
offer, I said to Mum and Dad that I would think it over. I explained
that I had met a charming young lady in Roscorla and life on the other
side of the English Channel was great.

The Conjuror

On a very cold January night I received an emergency call at 1.00am. A
heifer was having difficulty calving at Penhalligans, Higher Goonvean.
The senior partner gave me the map reference over the telephone. I
could see from the map that it was on a very bleak, exposed part of the
Moor near the famous Dozmary Pool. Local folklore decrees that as King
Arthur lay dying he ordered Bedevere to throw his famous sword,
Excalibur, into this lake. As this happened, a hand was reputed to

39

have come out of the water and grasped it. Thus it was returned to the
Lady of the Lake.

I drove to the farm as quickly as possible. I made fair speed along
the main A30 as far as the Jamaica Inn. The celebrated Blackbeard the
Pirate sign was swinging and creaking in the breeze as I turned off
into the winding country lane. Progress was slower along the much-
rutted track that led to the farm. The three Penhalligans,
grandfather, father and son, were anxiously waiting for me in the
farmyard, sheltering from the bitterly cold east wind in their
Landrover.

''er's out on the Moor, you!' Mr Penhalligan senior announced. 'You
cannae drive there, vetinree, you'll have to come wid thee. Us'll
'ave a churn full of hot water in the back. You'll need to bring your
torch. There be no light.' I grabbed some obstetrical equipment and
jumped into the Landrover. The four of us set off on the bumpy ride
across the Moor.

The outline of a shaggy coated heifer (a belted Galloway) could just be
seen by the light of the full moon. Her head was secured by a rope
halter attached to a ring in an oak post that had been sunk deep into
the ground inside a ramshackle wooden stockade. The heifer was very
agitated and snorting nervously. This hardy breed of cattle is rarely
handled. They are ideally suited to the rigours of the Moor. As we
approached she tried to escape, pulling back on the rope halter, her
eyes sticking out like organ stops.

'Her's proper mazed, you,' the middle Mr Penhalligan, pronounced.
Whilst wriggling into my parturition gown, Mr Penhalligan junior
asserted, 'Her's assafore, you.'

During one of our meetings in the pub, the vets had explained how
moorland farmers classified the various obstetrical mal-presentations.
I had learned from my colleagues that when the calf is coming backwards
the farmers would say, 'Tis backsifore, you.'

If the presentation were a breach (just like the calving case at Mr
O'Sullivan from Upper Ballymucklekill, near Tullymuck) they would say,
'Tis assafore, you'.

It was so cold I could barely move my fingers. Periodically, I had to
plunge my frozen hands and arms into the hot water in the milk churn to
enable me to move my fingers. The wind seemed to be coming straight
from Siberia. As I inserted my arms into the heifer's vagina, I was
expecting to feel a calf's tail, in view of Mr Penhaligan's comment.
To my surprise what I did feel were two feet, but no tail. I knew they
were front feet, since I could feel both fetlock and knee joints (both
joints flexed in the same direction). However, I could not feel the
calf's head. It was bent right back. I secured both front fetlock
joints with calving ropes - remembering my mentor Paddy McCooey and his
famous expression: 'What you have you hold.' Having applied copious
quantities of lubricant, I prayed that the heifer would not strain as I
pushed the calf back into the depths of the uterus. This procedure
just enabled me to manoeuvre the calf's head around into the pelvis.
Then I secured the head by attaching a rope around the base of the
ears. A small wooden pole was tied to each of the three ropes to

enable the Penhalligans to pull in turn, thus enabling them to apply traction to the head and each front leg. Now that the mal-presentation had been corrected, the delivery was relatively straightforward. The heifer was soon enthusiastically licking her calf - a bull, alive and kicking.

As I warmed myself beside the huge ash logs blazing in the inglenook fireplace in the farmhouse kitchen, I could see Mr Penhalligan senior was impatient to show me something, since he was a conjuror - an expert to boot. Coins magically disappeared and reappeared. Card tricks were his speciality. I could not see how he did them. It was legerdemain par excellence. These party-pieces were obviously his speciality. The tricks continued late into the night. Dawn was breaking as I left Higher Goonvean. It would be time for breakfast before I reached the hotel.

The indomitable Mrs Wonnacott

One late winter's morning, just as dawn was breaking, I received an urgent call to attend a South Devon cow at Wonnacotts, Polmassick and Warleggan on Bodmin Moor. I drove as quickly as I could. The cow had just calved, having given birth to a large live bull calf. Due to the strain of calving, the entire uterus had prolapsed. Everything I needed was ready: a metal bucket full of clean warm water, together with soap and towel. The large cow was lying in a deep bed of straw, in a loose box, constantly straining. I could sense from the general atmosphere that all was not well. The two huge Wonnacott men - father and son - were there, but neither of them said a word.

'We'll have to get her rear end up hill,' I said to Mr Wonnacott senior, 'so that we can work with the assistance of gravity.' He went as white as a sheet and fainted. I turned to his son to ask if he would help me move his father away from the cow (Mr Wonnacott senior was stretched out beside the cow, lying flat on his back in the straw). The son's complexion changed to a peculiar shade of duck-egg green, as he collapsed in the corner of the loose box. What was I to do? This was not the type of job the vet could do without help.

I hurriedly went into the granite farmhouse to see if anyone else was available to help. Mrs Wonnacott was busy in the kitchen cooking breakfast. She was a very small woman, no more than five feet tall. As I walked through the kitchen door, she gave me a knowing look. I felt she knew precisely what I was going to say. Before I had a chance to speak, she had rolled up her sleeves.

'I suppose they have given up the ghost. They always throw in the towel before they've even started,' she lamented, in a matter of fact, no nonsense fashion. With much hustle and bustle, she led the way across the farmyard towards the loose box.

Mrs Wonnacott was every veterinary surgeon's dream come true. 'What's to do, vetinree? You tell me zackly and I tell 'ee, 'twill be done,' she said reassuringly. If ever a woman meant business, it was the intrepid little Mrs Wonnacott, who might not have been very tall but she certainly was no quitter. I injected local anaesthetic into the epidural space of the cow's spine to ease the pain and stop her

41

straining. Mr Wonnacott senior was still unconscious, lying stretched
out on his back, alongside the recumbent cow.
'We can't just leave him lying there like that, vetineree,' Mrs
Wonnacott suddenly declared. ''E beez in the way!'
The two of us dragged the large man (a completely dead weight) as best
we could, across the floor of the loose box, and dumped him
unceremoniously in the corner beside Mr Wonnacott junior. Now that we
had cleared the decks, I could see by the determined look on Mrs
Wonnacott's face that she was anxious to get on with the job. By this
time the cow had rolled over and was now lying stretched out on her
side.
'Do you have some clean sheets please, Mrs Wonnacott?' I enquired.
As quick as a flash, the requested clean sheets duly appeared and one
was carefully placed under the cow's uterus to protect it. I slowly
but gently removed the afterbirth from the uterus. I meticulously
picked off all the pieces of straw which were sticking to the uterus.
The huge prolapsed organ, completely engorged with blood, was now
cleaned with water and disinfectant. Copious amounts of lubricant were
applied to it. Mrs Wonnacott was kneeling beside me in the straw,
poised and ready for action.
'You will have to help me to push the uterus back inside the cow by
using your clenched fists. First we will have to try to raise it, so
that we are not working against gravity. Do you have anything suitable
that would do the job?' I asked.
Mrs Wonnacott disappeared and in an instant magically returned with a
large wooden triangular wedge-shaped structure that she used for
raising heavy sacks of potatoes and milk churns. It was ideal. I
placed a clean sheet over it and pushed the sheeted wedge under the
prolapsed organ and raised it.
'Now we have gravity on our side,' I sighed, with relief.
With the two of us kneeling in the straw, we slowly but patiently
pushed the uterus back inside the cow with our fists. I pushed my arm
into the depths of the cow's uterus to make sure that it was totally
inverted. It was. Mrs Wonnacott's help had been invaluable. I
inserted a few pessaries into the uterus to combat infection and also
administered an injection of antibiotics into the cow's muscle as a
further precaution. A corticosteroid injection was given for shock.
Now that the uterus had been returned to its normal position inside the
abdomen, some pituitary extract was injected to make it shrink. I
attached a rope halter to the cow's head. With Mrs Wonnacott's help, I
managed to pull the cow's head up and roll her onto her sternum,
manoeuvring both her front and hind legs underneath her with
considerable difficulty.
'We will need some bales of straw to place beside her to keep her
upright. If you show me where they are, I will carry them,' I said.
We soon had the cow propped up with the bales of straw. The job was
almost complete. Despite all the shock to the system, the cow's pulse
was strong and the mucous membrane of the eye was surprisingly the
normal salmon pink colour. There did not appear to be any rupturing of
the vitally important uterine arteries.

An Irish vet looks back
by Fergus Ferguson ©

'What shall we do about your two men folk, Mrs Wonnacott?' I asked, pointing to the two farmers sleeping peacefully in the corner of the loose box.
'You leave 'em be, vetinree. Us'll go indoors and thee can eat their breakfast!'
Half an hour later, replete after a double helping of breakfast, we went to inspect the three patients. To our amazement, the cow was already on her feet, contentedly suckling her calf. However, the two men's progress was not so good. Mrs Wonnacott sighed, walked across and shook them both until they woke up.
Now fully recovered, Mr Wonnacott senior opened his eyes and stared at the cow. 'How did 'ee manage to do that, vetinree?' he queried.
'Necessity is the mother of invention,' I replied, heading for my motorcar.

Lambing time

The lambing season was well underway. I have always loved the springtime. It is a time of rebirth. Everything is new. Birds were singing. Ephemeral snowdrops had come and gone. Frogs had finished making their peculiar croaking courting calls. Village ponds were awash with frogspawn. Golden daffodils were in full bloom. Fragrant primroses were out in abundance in the huge Cornish banks on both sides of the moorland lanes. I had yet to hear the cuckoo, the harbinger of spring. It would soon be bluebell time.
In those days, the vets visited the farms for lambings. It was great fun. Sometimes the assistant would perform over twenty lambings in a day. The farms had been allocated map references. All calls were sent to the vet's motor car by radio-telephone from a control centre at the surgery. It was an extremely efficient system - very different from the informal mode of communication at Tullymuck. It is a wonderful feeling for a vet to be able to deliver a live lamb, sometimes in a field beside the daffodils. I have always considered it a great privilege to bring the newborn of any species into the world. It is an extremely invigorating experience and makes me feel very close to nature. The farmers, generally speaking, did not attempt obstetrical intervention - at least not on Bodmin Moor. If there was a problem, they took the view that it was the domain of the 'vetineree'.
The moorland scenery was breathtaking. Granite-built farmhouses and outbuildings with slate roofs were scattered about in isolated parts of the Moor. Ugly modern farm buildings had not yet appeared. There were very few trees. Any trees that existed were grossly misshapen, twisted and bent double by the remorseless and sometimes severe south-westerly wind. The sheep frequently lambed in the stone barns but, subject to the weather conditions, were soon turned out on the Moor after lambing for an early bite of spring grass. They had to find shelter for themselves on the leeward side of the huge hedges - earthen banks faced with local stone, with gorse and brambles growing on top. There were many meandering, lisping brooks on the Moor. The old granite stone bridges over these streams were a delight to see.

Staggers

Grass tetany or Staggers in beef suckling cattle was very common on
Bodmin Moor. This was an extremely serious disease of the central
nervous system, brought on by a dramatic drop in blood magnesium
levels. Suddenly the cows would start to twitch without warning and
frequently became incoordinate. In severe cases, they would totally
collapse in a fit. The vet had to attend as quickly as possible.
Convulsions were controlled by a barbiturate injection given
intravenously. This procedure was not easy to effect due to the
violent spasm. Magnesium sulphate was administered by subcutaneous
injection via a flutter valve. It could not be given intravenously
(except in a dire emergency) since, by using that mode of
administration, a too sudden increase of blood magnesium levels might
stop the heart. It was always a race against time. It took about
twenty minutes for the magnesium to be absorbed from under the skin.
This, together with the calming effect of the barbiturate, frequently
saved the cow's life. Sometimes the cow died before the vet arrived.
Worse still, in an extreme case, the cow died during treatment. It was
very worrying for both farmer and vet alike. Some vets transfused the
magnesium solution into the peritoneal cavity in an attempt to raise
the blood magnesium levels more quickly. This was more dangerous than
the subcutaneous route, but saved vital time.
Demelza Trelawney from Boscawen farm was a widow. She was assisted by a
farm labourer, called Cardew, who lived in a small granite cottage on
the farm. Demelza Trelawney was bent double from years of hard labour
on the land. Cardew was not much better since his knees had given out
from years of sheep shearing and lifting heavy hessian sacks of grain
hoisted onto his shoulders. Demelza originated from fisherfolk who
lived near Carn Les Boel at the Lizard Peninsula. Cardew's ancestors
were tin miners from the north Cornwall coast.
I responded to an emergency call on the radiotelephone since the
message was that one of their "bullocks" was flat out on the grass. 'I
will be there as quickly as I can.' I said. Demelza's and Cardew's
weather-beaten worried faces greeted me as I drove along the rough
track to Boscawen. They knew that from years of seeing similar cases
that the case would be touch and go.
The large North Devon "bullock" was flat out on the ground, frothing at
the mouth and paddling with all four feet. I manoeuvred a stiff rope
halter over her horns and secured the halter over her nose and neck,
tightening it around her head and passed the shank of the halter to
Cardew for him to hold, in an attempt to gain some control of the
spasms. I knew that the heart could stop at any time if the magnesium
fell to a critical level. I could take a chance and inject a solution
of magnesium sulphate into the jugular vein and this might save her
life. On the other hand, the vet was not supposed to inject any
magnesium into the bloodstream since this in itself might cause the
heart to stop beating. I was on the horns of a dilemma.
I could see that both Demelza and Cardew had a soft spot for Morwenna.
I tried to be masterful but in reality my heart was racing. 'I am going
to inject some Magnesium sulphate into her jugular vein otherwise she
might soon die from heart failure.' I announced, trying to look

44

confident. I have to warn you that this magnesium injected into the bloodstream itself might cause heart failure. By the look of her, if I inject the magnesium into the peritoneal cavity, or under her skin, it will take too long to raise the blood level of magnesium and Morwenna will die anyway. 'Hold tight onto the halter and try to keep her head steady, Cardew, while I inject this barbiturate into the jugular vein.' I declared, nervously. The barbiturate calmed the muscular spasms and this gave Morwenna some relief.

I decided to inject the magnesium sulphate solution into Morwenna's jugular vein even though I knew that the risks were high whichever course I took. Halfway through the magnesium injection, Morwenna suddenly stopped twitching and it looked to Demelza and Cardew that Morwenna was dead. I touched her cornea and she didn't blink. I listened to her heart and could not hear anything. I pinched her rectum and there was no reflex response. Morwenna was very definitely dead. This was the first case of an animal that that had died during treatment. It affected me very badly. I knew that Demelza was scratching a living from the land and the loss of a young beef "bullock" would be a major financial loss. An air of despondency descended over Boscawen farm. Demelza said bravely to me, 'Us knew there'd be a risk of death no matter which way thee gave the magnesium, vetinree.'

With a heavy heart, I thought it best if I should leave Boscawen.

Tyrone amongst the bushes

A veterinary surgeon in Kilcoot, County Tyrone, Ireland was in difficulty and urgently needed help. He knew my family. He was a racing enthusiast and frequently met up with his colleague, Roderick Fitzherbert of Drumlister House, for a day at the races. I can only surmise that Mr Fitzherbert had suggested I might be able to come to his rescue. The decision to leave Bodmin Moor and Kate was not an easy one. Admittedly, I was missing the green fields of Ireland. I had become attached to the moorland farmers and their quaint ways. The Cornish countryside in spring was particularly beautiful.

After much soul-searching, I decided to pack my bags and head for Ireland. County Tyrone, for some strange reason, has always been affectionately referred to by country people as "Tyrone amongst the bushes". It was late springtime and the ewes were still lambing.

Houdini

On my first evening on duty in Kiloot, a farmer telephoned in a panic, saying he had a ewe that was having difficulty lambing. Before I had a chance to ask his name, he announced that he and the ewe were on their way to the surgery, and replaced the receiver.

I waited patiently in the surgery, expecting a Landrover to arrive. When a battered, old black car pulled into the yard, I did not pay too much attention to it. I continued doing my bookings. Suddenly there was a loud thumping on the surgery door and a red-faced farmer burst in.

'Where's the vet?' he demanded. 'I thought you'd be standing in the yard waiting for me to come!'

Realising that this must be my client, I replied, 'I'm the vet. I was watching out for a Landrover. Where's the ewe?'

An Irish vet looks back
by Fergus Ferguson ©

'She's in the boot!' he replied. 'Come and take a look at her. The lamb's head is out and it's nearly dead!' I followed him quickly to the car. This was the first time I had come across a ewe transported in a motor car. The boot-lid was half-heartedly secured. Several lengths of baler twine were tied around the boot handle and attached to the rear bumper in a haphazard fashion. The boot lid was ajar and the baler twine was not taut. The farmer drew a penknife from his pocket, opened it and hurriedly cut through the lengths of twine. Lifting the boot-lid, to our amazement, there was no sign of the ewe.

'Bejabers, she's disappeared!' Without further ado, he slammed the boot-lid shut, leapt into the driving seat and drove off out of the yard, crashing the gears as he went. I never discovered his name. That was the last I saw of him.

Nature works in mysterious ways

On a subsequent evening, I received a call from a very excited farmer informing me that his ewe needed a Caesarean operation. It was agreed that he should bring the ewe to the surgery immediately. On examination, the ewe appeared to be on the point of lambing, she was bagged up, i.e. she had a full udder and was running milk. Breathing very heavily she seemed quite distressed. Her vulva was extremely swollen and was severely bruised, presumably as a consequence of previous attempts at lambing. It was impossible to ascertain whether or not the cervix or neck of the womb was dilated; the vagina was so swollen, I was unable to carry out an internal examination.

In situations like this the vet has to be very careful. Prior intervention by farmers sometimes causes the death of the lambs. Also, the ewe's uterus may be ruptured, causing death from peritonitis and shock.

The fiery, large-framed farmer with a ruddy weather-beaten face had a mindset; the only way forward was for me to perform a Caesarean section. Were the lambs alive or dead? I could not tell. In a futile attempt to protect myself, I pointed to the swollen, bruised, discoloured vulva and said, 'I see that someone has tried to lamb her.' The farmer exploded, treating my concern with utter contempt: 'I tell you, vet, she hasn't been interfered with at all, at all, at all!' It was clear from his stance that all veterinary appeals to logic and reasonableness would be treated with disdain, even though it was patently obvious that earlier obstetrical manoeuvres had taken place. With considerable reluctance and apprehension I agreed to carry out the Caesarean section as requested. The large black-faced Suffolk ewe was secured on her side on the practice operating table. Her flank was anaesthetised with local anaesthetic, clipped, shaved and disinfected, in readiness for abdominal surgery. An incision was made through the ewe's skin, muscle layers, peritoneum and the abdominal cavity was entered. The uterus was exteriorised and a further incision made through the uterine wall. The first lamb lifted from the uterus was very much alive and kicking. It bleated plaintively for its mother. The second lamb was in the normal position - head and front feet first, right down in its mother's pelvis. I grabbed it by its hind legs and extricated it from the ewe's womb. It had obviously been dead for some

An Irish vet looks back
by Fergus Ferguson ©

time since its head was very swollen and blue. More interestingly,
each front leg had brightly-coloured orange baler twine tied just above
the fetlock joint. Despite his earlier protestations to the contrary,
it was obvious (to me, at least) that antecedent obstetrical
interventions had taken place.
Having removed the orange baler twine from the dead lamb's front legs,
I handed him the controversial item, commenting: 'Nature works in
mysterious ways!' The colour drained from his face. Looking decidedly
disconcerted, he hurriedly secreted the controversial baler twine in
his coat pocket. Not a word was spoken as I completed the operation.
TVO poisoning
I had just returned to the surgery, having finished my morning rounds.
An urgent call to visit a goat awaited me. Mr O'Gorman had reported
that his goat had suddenly started to walk round and round in circles.
When I arrived in the potholed yard, he directed me to a dark,
tumbledown wooden hovel, with a low corrugated iron roof. The goat, a
seven year old billy - a large hairy animal with a magnificent pair of
straight pointed horns and a thick grey beard - was walking clockwise
in an uncontrollable fashion around his living quarters. It was
explained that Rafferty was the local stud goat whose services were
required the length and breadth of the entire locality.
My initial diagnosis was that he might have developed meningitis, his
brain seemed to be affected. Mr O'Gorman grabbed him by his beard and
horns to restrain him. During my clinical examination, I noticed that
the hair was flattened over his entire body. Some type of greasy
substance seemed to have been applied. It had a distinct oleaginous
smell. It was surprising that my nose could detect any smell above the
ghastly offensive aroma associated with uncastrated goats. There were
several circular hairless skin lesions on both flanks, the neck and
face, which looked suspiciously like the fungal disease known to
country people as ringworm. In view of the unknown nature of the oily
material, I felt that it was time to pause and reflect. Mr O'Gorman
released the goat and leaned against the manger, his body language was
extremely defensive - legs crossed, arms akimbo. Instinctively, I felt
that some home-made or other concoction might have been used to treat
the ringworm; I was beginning to wonder whether this could account for
Rafferty's unusual behaviour. The application of proprietary lotions
was quite common but farmers were, perhaps understandably, reluctant to
admit to it.
'I think Rafferty has ringworm. Have you applied anything to his skin
to treat it?' I enquired, tentatively. I could see that Mr O'Gorman
was extremely reluctant to answer my question. I knew from my student
days that extracting such information from a farmer would be harder
than pulling teeth.
Mr O'Gorman shuffled from one foot to another, removed his cap,
scratched his head and replaced the cap at an oblique angle. 'I'd
better come clean vet. Last night I was in McGuire's pub," admitting
that he had been telling anyone who cared to listen about Rafferty's
ringworm and asking all the neighbours how to cure it. Innumerable
remedies had been tendered. One farmer, who had been the worse for

An Irish vet looks back
by Fergus Ferguson ©

wear, swore blind that the application of TVO (tractor vaporising oil)
was guaranteed to work. Impressed by this cheap, handy copper-bottomed
cure, Mr O'Gorman had decided to give it a go. It seemed to me that
Rafferty may have tried to lick this offensive material off his coat
and might have ingested a considerable quantity. Alternatively, it
might have been absorbed through the skin, or maybe both.
'You'll have to wash his coat thoroughly with detergent,' I instructed
Mr O'Gorman, 'to try to remove all traces of the oil. In cases like
this, where there is no specific antidote, I will give him a
multivitamin injection intravenously to try to detoxify the system.
This should assist the metabolism of the liver by enabling this organ
to remove the poisonous substance.'
Rafferty was standing quietly beside his hay net, contentedly chewing
the cud. However, the ringworm was still present and some veterinary
treatment was supplied.
I had never heard about TVO poisoning in any animal, let alone a goat,
and wondered whether it would be a suitable case for publication in the
Veterinary Record.
Lightning strike
During the following week there had been a violent overnight storm.
Large trees had been uprooted and blown to the ground. The thunder and
lightning had disturbed my slumbers. Next morning, a farmer telephoned
to say that two of his heavyweight hunter horses had escaped into the
road and had been killed by a passing lorry. A required a veterinary
certificate was required, to enable him to make an insurance claim to
compensate him for his loss.
When I arrived, Mr Murphy was very agitated. As prearranged, I met him
in the lane, he demanded that I certify the cause of death. "Spud"
Murphy was a very formidable gentleman, clearly used to getting his own
way, he was not the type of man to be trifled with. On arrival at the
scene, I found the horses, a dark brown gelding and a liver chestnut
mare, stretched out side by side on the wide grass verge, beside the
metalled carriageway. Neither horse was breathing nor moving. It was
obvious that they were both dead. Following a careful examination, I
noticed, amongst other things, that both horses were shod on all four
feet. I could see no evidence of external trauma to either horse.
There was no sign of skid marks, either on the carriageway or the grass
verge. However, what I did observe was a considerable length of
freshly flattened grass along the wide verge that led directly to the
horses. I was beginning to smell a rat. I walked along the lane
beside the flattened grass and noted that it commenced at a gap in the
hedge. I peered through the gap and could see that the trail led all
the way to a large oak tree standing in the middle of the field.
Interestingly and significantly, wheel marks clearly made by a tractor
could be seen in the grass, stretching from the oak tree to the hole in
the hedge.
Slowly but surely the penny was beginning to drop. It seemed far more
plausible that the two horses might have been killed by lightning while
standing under the oak tree, rather than the result of a road traffic
accident, as asserted by Mr Murphy. During inclement weather, horses

instinctively huddle together under the lee of hedges or trees to protect themselves from the driving rain. A bolt of lightning frequently strikes a tree in the middle of a field and is subsequently earthed through the metal horseshoes. All country folk know that neither people nor animals should shelter under a tree during a thunderstorm. When I was a boy, my uncle's neighbour lost several bullocks from lightning strike, as they stood under some trees during a storm.

I knew that "lightning strike" in insurance law was categorised as an act of God and, as such, was an express exclusion clause of any contract. I felt certain that Spud was only too aware of this fact. Accordingly, the horses had been dragged across the field to the side of the road, to make it appear as if they had been involved in a road traffic accident. What was I to do? I could not issue an untrue veterinary certificate. Such an act would be a conspiracy to defraud the insurance company. This was the first time in my professional career that I had been put to the test. The devious Mr Murphy had remained beside the horses. He had been watching my every move like a hawk. When I returned, I could see that he had adopted a hostile stance.

'Are you going to issue the certificates, vet? ' he snarled, threateningly. 'If you don't, I will have to summon another vet. There's plenty of others who will!'

I did not like his menacing attitude, nor what I was being asked to do. I summoned all the courage I could muster, pulled myself up to my full height and tried to be as self-assertive as possible.

'Mr Murphy, in my professional opinion there is no evidence whatsoever that your horses have been involved in a road traffic accident. It is my view that they may have been killed by lightning during last night's thunderstorm. I cannot issue the certificates which you have requested. If you wish to seek the services of another veterinary surgeon that, of course, is your prerogative. Good-day to you.'

I jumped into my car and drove away as quickly as possible. I was trembling with fear. I did not realise it at the time but this decision was to hold me in good stead for the rest of my professional career.

Risus sardonicus - the farmer with lockjaw

My next call was to visit a cow which needed a "looking away" injection. In certain parts of Ireland, when a cow is in season and receptive to the bull, she is said to be looking away. Sammy Sweeney from Drumclamp lived on a small farm with his mother. A bachelor, he had been conscientiously watching his cow for weeks, but she had shown no signs of coming into season. In appropriate cases, the vet would administer a hormone injection to the cow, which subsequently made her receptive to the advances of the bull.

Following the consultation, Sammy invited me indoors for a cup of tea, he was wearing an open-necked shirt. I could see a large scar on his throat and, from its precise location, it seemed to me that it might have been the result of a tracheotomy. I asked Sammy if he would mind telling me whether he had had an operation on his neck. Without any embarrassment whatever, Sammy told me that he had suffered from lockjaw, or tetanus, a few years ago. I had never spoken to anyone who had recovered from lockjaw, so I was all ears. I had seen the disease in animals on numerous occasions but had had no experience of it in man.

One day while working on the farm, Sammy had cut his hand badly with a crosscut saw in the V-shaped depression between his index finger and thumb. The wound had become infected but he had stubbornly refused to visit the doctor. Two weeks later, he had become unwell, and had had difficulty in chewing and swallowing, Sammy's facial appearance changed and his Mother was becoming very concerned about him, she insisted that he visit the surgery. Sammy described his symptoms to the doctor who, although realising that there was a serious problem, could not make a definitive diagnosis. Sammy was sent straight away to see the consultant at the nearby hospital. After examining Sammy, the consultant listened to all the details concerning his wound and his present difficulties with chewing and swallowing, he too was also unable to make a definite diagnosis or to find anything the matter with Sammy's mouth. Sammy was then referred to the oral surgical department of the hospital to have his teeth checked. No signs of dental or gum disease were discovered and Sammy was sent home, where his condition continued to deteriorate. Sammy's mother became increasingly alarmed, as he was becoming quite stiff and was having difficulty in moving. The next night whilst trying to drink a cup of tea, Sammy's facial expression changed dramatically, his features became drawn due to spasm of the muscles of his forehead and face. This exposed his teeth, giving his countenance the peculiar expression known as <u>risus sardonicus</u> (the sardonic grin). In desperation, his Mother decided they would have to visit their old family friend - a retired doctor. Hitching the trap to the pony, she helped Sammy into the seat. They set off along the lanes in search of Dr O'Leary. By the time they arrived darkness had fallen. The elderly doctor had already retired for the night, on hearing the clip clop of the pony's shoes as they drove into his yard and realised that there must be some sort of crisis.

When he heard the sorry tale, he took one look at Sammy and said: 'My God, its lockjaw!' Fortunately for Sammy, Dr O'Leary had been a surgeon in the Royal Army Medical Corps in India and had seen many previous cases of tetanus. Sammy was immediately taken by ambulance to the Royal Victoria Hospital in Belfast. By the time he arrived in the intensive care unit, opisthotonos had developed. In this state, the patient's body assumes a bent backward attitude, due to severe periodic muscular spasms of the spine. A general anaesthetic was given, together with a muscle relaxant drug, to control the spasm, placed on a ventilator, since as a result of the muscle relaxant drug, he was unable to breathe for himself. This was why Sammy had the tracheotomy, since he told me that the drug that they used to control the spasms was the same drug which the South American Indians use in their blow darts for paralysing their prey. I believe it was probably the drug known as curare.

An Irish vet looks back
by Fergus Ferguson ©

For twelve weeks Sammy's life had been in the balance, since he was
unable to move a muscle and he was kept alive by liquids fed to him by
stomach tube and intravenous drip. Sammy had had a narrow escape.
Luckily, he made a complete recovery.
Sammy was a very keen football enthusiast. On the day of the FA
Football Final, his mother came to visit him in hospital. Although he
could not move a muscle and was unable to communicate with her in any
way, the medical staff explained that apart from when he was asleep, he
was fully conscious. Just before his mother left his side, she made
sure that the bedside radio was turned on to the big match, to enable
him to hear it after she had gone. Part way through the match the
consultant and his entourage came to examine Sammy. The nurse turned
off the radio. Unfortunately, when the consultation was finished, she
forgot to turn on the radio again - much to Sammy's chagrin, he had
always regretted being unable to hear the rest of the match. It was
not until sometime later, when he had almost recovered, that he learned
the result.

Bob and Nellie - an island farm in Lough Erne

Some of the more distant clients, on the western side of the practice,
farmed along the shores of Lough Erne in County Fermanagh. It is a
very large inland lake. People say there are 365 islands in Lough Erne
- one for every day of the year. It is known locally as the Lake
District of Ireland. Situated towards the west of Ireland, it has a
very high rainfall. In the wintertime, the water level in the lough
rises considerably. Country people would say that Lough Erne was in
Fermanagh in the summer but Fermanagh was in Lough Erne in the winter.
Most of the islands were uninhabited. Herds of wild goats swam from
island to island in search of fresh grass. The wildlife was fantastic:
otters, kingfishers and, in particular, water-loving birds, such as
great crested grebe. The huge salmon from the Atlantic Ocean came up
the fast flowing river Erne to spawn in the calm fresh waters of the
Lough. The fishing was wonderful. The undulating dark blue Donegal
Mountains could be seen in the distance, beyond the shores of the
Lough.
The telephone rang, it was well after midnight. Bertie Gill farmed on
the shores of the lough. I had met him once before, as he recounted
that his neighbour's sow could not "pig". In certain parts of Ireland,
when a sow is farrowing, for some peculiar reason she is said to be
"pigging". Also, the "piglets" are referred to as "wee pigs".
Explaining that his neighbour was an elderly bachelor who lived in a
thatched cottage on a small island about half a mile from the shore.
Bertie had been to see him earlier that evening, since he knew that the
sow was about to pig - for some time now he had been keeping a
neighbourly eye on him and helping with his animals. Bertie arranged
to meet me at the nearest cross roads to the Lough shore.
As I drew up at the crossroads, I could see Bertie standing on the
leeward side of a thick hawthorn hedge, holding a hurricane lamp.
Bertie had explained on the telephone that we would have to travel to

the island by boat. Introductions over, I placed the necessary
equipment in my bag. Bertie held the lamp aloft as led the way along
the path to the Lough shore, asking me to hold the hurricane lamp as he
rowed sedately across the still waters towards the island. During the
crossing, Bertie explained that his neighbour Bob lived with his
elderly housekeeper, Nellie, who had originally come from County
Donegal. They had met many years ago at a hiring fair. Consistent
with local custom, Nellie had been hired for a year. By mutual
agreement she remained there ever since. As we approached the island,
I began to see the outline of a collection of thatched whitewashed
buildings. The stout trunk of a willow tree was used as a secure
mooring for the boat. We clambered out of the boat and up the slight
slope from the waters edge to the farm yard.
Bob Buchanon was waiting anxiously by his cottage door. The fire was
burning brightly in the kitchen behind him. By the light of the
paraffin lamp, I could see Nellie was lifting the kettle of boiling
water off the crook. Pouring it into a metal bucket she carried it
outside to the piggery, together with soap and towel. A hurricane lamp
was suspended from a beam above the sow, her udder was congested and
she was running milk, and straining unproductively. Pigging cases were
not uncommon in that particular breed - a Large White sow. I knelt
down on the deep bed of straw to examine the sow. It was immediately
apparent that there was a pig stuck in her pelvis. I lubricated the
vagina. There was just sufficient room to enable me to deliver the
pig. Unfortunately it was dead. On further internal examination, I
could feel another pig descending into the pelvis. I gave the sow two
injections in the muscle of the neck: some pituitary extract to make
the uterus contract and penicillin to prevent metritis. Usually in a
case of this nature, once the offending pig is removed, all is well. I
always liked to wait to make sure that the sow managed to give birth to
at least one further pig on her own.
Bob invited us into the kitchen for a cup of tea. In anticipation,
Nellie had wet the tea and was busily spreading home-made butter on the
soda bread which she had made earlier in the day.
We sat down on the high-backed settles on either side of the fire.
After tea, both Bob and Bertie lit their pipes. Nellie also smoked a
pipe. It was a thin, white clay pipe with a long stem and had a much
more delicate bowl than the men's pipes. Many Donegal women smoked
clay pipes. Like so many women of her generation, Nellie was clothed
in black from head to foot. As all three smoked contentedly around the
fire, they regaled me with stories about life on the islands in Lough
Erne. Bertie explained that in the wintertime the cattle stayed on the
mainland. As soon as the grass began to grow in the springtime, the
cattle were moved to the nearest uninhabited island. It was
fascinating to learn how this was achieved. A goat was tethered to the
back of a boat. A man in the boat would then row towards the island
with the goat forced to swim along behind. The herd of cattle was
driven into the water. Goats being very good swimmers, would happily
swim on the tether behind the boat. Cattle are also very proficient at
swimming. Once they had been driven into the water, it was not too

difficult to persuade the cattle to follow the goat. Farmers know from
experience that they can take advantage of cattle's natural herding
extinct. Once cattle start to swim they will always follow the animal
in front of them. The islands varied in size from less then half an
acre to several acres. Once the grass had been eaten, the swimming was
then repeated; thus moving them to a new island for fresh grazing,
throughout the summer months. So far as I could ascertain, this simple
island-hopping procedure had been going on since time immemorial.
Bob suggested that I might like to hire a boat and explore the islands.
He gave me a cautionary word of warning. If I wanted to explore any of
the islands, I should be wary of the billy-goats since they had very
long horns and were extremely aggressive and dangerous. Apparently, it
was quite likely that they would lower their heads and charge straight
at anyone who came anywhere near them. He also suggested that I might
like to visit the mysterious pagan, carved stone figures on Boa and
White Islands. The famous Round Tower on nearby Devinish Island was
said to have been built as a means of escape for the local people since
the marauding Vikings frequently came up the river Erne in their long
boats.
As I stared into the dying embers in the early hours of the morning, I
felt as if I was in a time warp. I had to shake myself: I was supposed
to be dealing with a serious obstetrical emergency. When we returned
to the piggery, fortunately all was well. The sow had given birth to
one dozen pigs, she was stretched out on her side in the straw and the
pigs were all frantically jostling for a position to drink from the
large amount of milk that was flowing freely from her udder, she had
stopped straining. An internal examination revealed that she had
finished pigging. Her family was complete. Nellie said that the dead
pig was the unlucky one since it would have made a litter of thirteen.
I thanked Bob and Nellie for their kind hospitality and bade them
goodnight. On our way back to the mainland I asked Bertie if many of
the islands were still inhabited, he told me that the larger islands
were still working farms but the smaller islands had been abandoned.
Bob and Nellie were a dying breed. The island itself was only a few
acres in size. It supported a house cow, some pigs, sheep and goats
and a few chickens and geese. An idyllic setting in which to live, but
very isolated; the post could not be delivered during the severe winter
of 1963.
'I notice they are superstitious,' I said, referring to Nellie's
comment about the litter of thirteen.
'Oh, yes,' Bertie replied. 'People are very superstitious around here.
No one would ever cut down a fairy tree growing in the middle of a
field. It was guaranteed to bring seven years bad luck. A local man
defied the taboo and cut down a fairy tree in the middle of one of his
fields, he used the tree trunk as a stanchion in his byre. Every
single cow, which was tied to this post, died.'
The fairy tree is of course the hawthorn or quick thorn tree. Bertie
went on to tell me about a man in the next townland who was the seventh
son of a seventh son. Everyone believed that he had magical healing

powers. People suffering from a wide variety of diseases came from
miles around to be cured by his touch.
When we returned to the car, I offered Bertie a lift back to his
farmhouse, he politely declined saying that his loaning was just around
the corner and he welcomed the opportunity of a short walk before
retiring. He liked to watch the barn owls as they hunted along the
loaning and around the farm buildings. If he were lucky he might see
one.

Flowers of sulphur

Drew Beggs from Drumskinny was very mean, he rarely called the vet. If
he did so, it was only as a last resort. I had heard from neighbouring
farmers that the vet normally arrived just in time to administer the
last rites. All his beasts were coughing and losing weight and it
seemed obvious that they were suffering from husk pneumonia. This is a
parasitic disease of grazing cattle, which causes damage to the lungs
and windpipe. It occurs in summer and autumn. Drew had been asking
everyone in the locality what he could do or give them to avoid an
expensive visit from the vet. To placate him, the postman had told him
that heated flowers of sulphur might do the trick. Drew decided to try
this recommended remedy, placing a stove in the corner of a stone
building, he lit a fire. A metal bucket was placed with flowers of
sulphur and placed on the fire. Next he drove the coughing cattle into
the shed. Finally he shut all the doors and windows and carried on
with his chores.
A short time later he returned to see how they were getting on. On
peering through the window he was horrified to discover that several of
them had collapsed on the floor. They were all salivating profusely
and gasping for breath. He rushed into the shed, grabbed the fuming
bucket and carried it outside. What a quandary. Should he call the
vet? If he did nothing, all his stock might die. Alternatively, he
would have to pay: something which did not appeal to his parsimonious
nature.
I drove to Drumskinny as quickly as I could. When I arrived the beasts
were either lying stretched out on the ground in an extremely
distressed state or staggering around the yard. I could smell the
acrid fumes of the sulphur.
'What's going on?' I asked. There was no way out for Drew, who
confessed all.
With considerable difficulty we managed to raise all the beasts to
their feet and push them outside the shed into the fresh air. When I
realised what had happened, I was at a loss to know what to do. I had
never encountered anything like this before, either whilst training or
in practice. In cases of poisoning, three principles apply: remove the
animals from the source of the poison; administer a specific antidote,
if one is available; in the absence of a specific antidote, treat the
symptoms. To the best of my knowledge there was no specific antidote
to poisoning with the fumes of flowers of sulphur. Each beast was
given an anti-inflammatory injection in an attempt to relieve the
symptoms. Fortunately the distressed breathing abated shortly after

the injections were administered. I very much doubted that Drew's
unorthodox remedy had cured the original disease. I knew that I would
have to return again to administer an anti-parasitic injection when it
was safe to do so.
A few days later, I returned to inspect the beasts. They appeared to
have recovered from the effects of the flowers of sulphur but were all
still coughing as a consequence of the parasites migrating through
their lungs. Prompt action was required. They were all given an
injection to kill the lungworms. Fortunately, in due course, they all
made a complete recovery. Unfortunately, Drew's niggardly nature had
cost him dearly.

Netherzoy

My duties at Kilcoot were rapidly coming to an end. It was time for me
to find another locum appointment. I decided to refer once more to the
bundle of letters that I had received in response to my advertisement
in the Veterinary Record. The first letter I pulled out of the parcel
was from a Mr Matthew Swann who practised in the town of Netherzoy in
Somerset. A locum was urgently required to run a busy, single-handed,
mainly large animal practice. When I telephoned, Mrs Swann explained
that they still had not managed to find a locum. Their holiday was due
to start in a few days. I agreed to go.
The old nux vomica and the confidence trickster
Mrs Swann had arranged to meet me at the station at 3.30pm. It was
agreed that I would be holding a copy of The Veterinary Record. On the
way back to the surgery, Mrs Swann explained that the practice covered

a very large area. It extended from Glastonbury Tor, the Burrowbridge
Mump, the Quantock and Brendon Hills as far as Exmoor. The border of
the practice swept down through the Taunton Vale up into part of the
Blackdown Hills and included a large portion of the southern Somerset
levels to the east. We drew up behind a substantial town house set in
a large garden. The surgery was in the basement at the back of the
house. Mrs Swann gave me a quick tour of the house, then showed me to
my room.

'I'll put the kettle on. You must be in need of a cup of tea after
your long journey. After tea you can meet Matthew downstairs in the
surgery. He can show you around before dinner.' She disappeared
downstairs to the kitchen, while I unpacked my belongings.

'Tea's ready,' she called up from the bottom of the stairs. Over tea
and cake, she told me that their daughter Diana would be around to help
me. Apparently each vacation, when she came home from university,
Diana helped her father with the practice. In the long summer
vacation, she always helped the locum while her parents went abroad for
a fortnight. This would be her last opportunity to help, since she had
graduated in law, completed her pupillage and had been called to the
Bar. Diana had just returned from a holiday with friends in
Switzerland, as she was scheduled to spend two weeks at home before
joining a set of Chambers at Lincoln's Inn. I began to feel that I was
going to enjoy the next two weeks. The practice covered some beautiful
parts of the English countryside and, judging by the photographs I had
glimpsed on the baby grand piano on my cursory tour of the house, I
would have a delightful companion!

Although feeling refreshed after the welcoming tea in the kitchen, I
was still slightly nervous and apprehensive when Mrs Swann took me down
to the surgery to introduce me to her husband. Mr Swann was an
intimidating man - tall, handsome and greying at the temples. I felt
instinctively that he was not the type of man to suffer fools gladly.
Consultations finished for the evening, everything was neat and tidy.
Matthew Swann gave me a guided tour of the surgery and dispensary,
explaining where everything was kept. I was asked innumerable
questions, including how I would treat a case of water dropwort
poisoning in a cow and how I would deal with a dog with suspected
rabies. No employer had questioned me in such depth before. It felt
as if I was back at Trinity in the middle of an oral examination. I
was relieved when we were summoned to the sitting room for pre-dinner
drinks. The inquisition was at an end!

Tall, dark and slim, Diana had a figure that any woman would die for.
A holiday tan was shown off to its best advantage by an expensive
little black dress, her long dark hair shone as if it had been
polished. When Diana was introduced to me over a glass of sherry in
the sitting room, she exclaimed: 'Oh, you are much younger than I'd
expected! In previous years, Daddy has always had very much older vets
to help him.' I thought that this possibly explained her father's in-
depth questioning. Perhaps he was showing normal paternal concern:
such a young vet left alone with his beautiful daughter. Or did he
merely think that I had insufficient experience to cope with the

An Irish vet looks back
by Fergus Ferguson ©

rigours of single-handed practice? Perhaps it was an oblique hint that I must concentrate my efforts on the job in hand? There was no time to ponder. The barrage of questions started again.

'Fergus, I'm a little concerned,' said Mr Swann, peering directly at me over his horn-rimmed spectacles. 'Where did you say you studied?'

'Trinity College, Dublin, Sir,' I replied.

The interrogation continued. 'Which year did you qualify?'

'1965, Sir.'

A definite look of relief spread over his face. 'Ah! That may explain why I cannot find your name in the Veterinary Register. It is, of course, a biennial publication and your name should appear in the next edition. Where have you worked since you graduated?'

Mrs Swann seemed to sense my growing unease. Smiling, she pronounced, 'Diana, I think you had better put Fergus out of his misery. It's your story. Let's go through to the dining room. Over dinner you and your father can tell Fergus the long story about the last locum.'

Looking me straight in the eye, she asked: 'Have you ever heard of Jonathan Spencer-Wells? Perhaps not, being an Irishman. Most of Matthew's colleagues, here in the West Country, certainly have,' she said over her shoulder, as she led the way into the dining room.

Mr Swann described how he had placed his usual advertisement in the Veterinary Record for a locum to run his practice during his absence on holiday last year. A Mr Jonathan Spencer-Wells replied in writing, stating that he was available and willing to act as a locum. Mr Swann checked his entry in the Register of Veterinary Surgeons and realised that Mr Spencer-Wells had qualified a few years before him at London University. Not knowing him particularly well, he had a clear opinion of his personality and appearance. He felt that he could trust him to run the practice. Arrangements were confirmed by telephone and he arrived as agreed on the morning of the day of their departure on holiday. Mr Swann was slightly concerned on two points. First, Jonathan Spencer-Wells seemed to have changed considerably in appearance from the undergraduate he remembered from his student days. Mr Swann thought perhaps that he had mistaken him for someone else, since it was a long time ago and quite a large Faculty. Second, when he was giving him a conducted tour of the surgery and dispensary, Jonathan Spencer-Wells did not seem to relate to the various familiar drugs on the shelf as one would have expected from an experienced professional colleague. When Mr Swann showed him the nux vomica powders (a proprietary remedy which contained strychnine amongst other things), which was no longer in common everyday usage by the modern veterinary surgeon, Mr Spencer-Wells latched on to it, as if it were a long-lost friend, saying: 'Ah, the old nux vomica!' It appeared to Mr Swann that this was the only medicine with which he seemed to be familiar.

'I realise now, with the benefit of hindsight, that these two things should have set warning bells ringing.'

Diana then interjected, saying that she had been suspicious about Mr Spencer-Wells as soon as her parents had left as he did not seem to behave in the same way as any of the previous elderly locums, he would never talk about his past professional career and did not seem to know any of Daddy's friends. On the surface, he appeared to work very hard and seemed to deal with most of the cases reasonably well. Mr Spencer-Wells always seemed to proceed in a clandestine fashion. One of our regular farmers complained bitterly that he had made no attempt whatever to replace his cow's prolapsed uterus, simply advising him to have it slaughtered. I was alarmed to hear from the farmer that he had had to call in one of Daddy's colleagues, who replaced the cow's uterus.'

'Things came to a head on spay day. Daddy always arranges to castrate and spay the cats once a fortnight. I had mentioned this to Mr Spencer-Wells and had been booking them in as usual. I always helped Daddy with the anaesthetic. When spay day came, I admitted all the cats. I placed them in secure metal cat baskets, individually labelling each with their owners' names and addresses. Mr Spencer-Wells informed me that he normally preferred to attend to the operations without assistance. At the eleventh hour, he suddenly announced that he had some urgent business to attend to and would be away for a couple of hours. I was busy on the telephone arranging afternoon visits when I noticed him drive away from the premises. I went downstairs to the surgery to check the animals and was alarmed to note that they had all disappeared. Later in the day Mr Spencer-Wells returned. From the upstairs window I watched him surreptitiously carry all the cat baskets back into the surgery. Mr Spencer-Wells asked me for the list of afternoon calls and left. I went back downstairs to discover that all the cats had been spayed and castrated. They all appeared to be fit and well. I assumed that he had arranged to have the operations carried out by a nearby veterinary surgeon. Mummy and Daddy were coming home the next day, so I felt it was best for me to leave Daddy to deal with the matter.'

Mr Swann continued: 'We returned from holiday and Mr Spencer-Wells left. In the circumstances I was most concerned about his bona fides. I thought I had better raise the matter with the Secretary and Registrar at the Royal College of Veterinary Surgeons in Belgrave Square, London. The Registrar informed me that they had received several complaints about the nefarious activities of Mr Spencer-Wells. Apparently, the Mr Spencer-Wells whom I had known at College had retired and purchased a farmhouse in the Welsh hills, had died a short time later. [The Registrar of the RCVS is not necessarily informed every time a veterinary surgeon dies.] This man, realising that he could possibly exploit the situation, wrote to the Royal College of Veterinary Surgeons purporting to be Jonathan Spencer-Wells, advising them of his change of address. The RCVS acknowledged receipt of the letter, informing him that they had amended his particulars. In due course they sent him the standard reminder for the membership subscription, which, as you know, is paid annually on the 1st April. The confidence trickster, alias Mr Spencer-Wells, paid the subscription by return of post, confirming his particulars, together with his new address and telephone number. These were duly entered in the next edition of the Register of practising veterinary surgeons.'

Mrs Swann, realising that the air had now been cleared, suggested that everyone might like to return to the sitting room for coffee. Much to my great relief, the inquisition was finally over. I felt that Mr Swann had accepted that I would be a suitable locum, when he offered me a large brandy with my coffee.

During the course of the next two weeks, the clients regaled me with numerous stories about the antics of the notorious Mr Jonathan Spencer-Wells. Irrespective of ailment, he invariably prescribed a course of 'the old nux vomica' to be administered daily as a drench for a week. I reassured them that although I was young, I was fully qualified, was not bogus, and was definitely not mindful to prescribe nux vomica.

Bracken poisoning

One day I received an urgent call to visit a herd of some twenty fattening cattle, at grass in the Blackdown Hills. On arrival, two were dead. Blood was coming from various external orifices. Several of the other animals were unwell, all with high temperatures, some as high as 106. They were very depressed, off their food and breathing rapidly. Initially, I suspected Anthrax, but soon ruled this out when I discovered that they had been eating bracken. Bracken poisoning is quite rare. The stock was moved to safe pasture. The toxic ingredient in bracken interferes with the metabolism of the bone marrow, thereby making the animals susceptible to infection and prone to haemorrhage. I visited them daily to administer antibiotic and multivitamin injections and monitor their progress. Fortunately, they made a complete recovery.

It was a beautiful area in which to practise. The countryside varied enormously from one part of the practice to another. The scenery in the Brendon and Quantock Hills was magnificent. There were beautiful wooded hills and valleys everywhere. Exmoor, by contrast, was very open and exposed. This was the famous Lorna Doone country, immortalised by RD Blackmore. Huge earthen banks topped by stock proof beech hedges bordered the fields and the Moor. South Wales could be seen in the distance, across the Severn Estuary. The sheltered Taunton Vale was a different world from the exposed and wind-swept Exmoor. The soil in the Vale was very fertile - a characteristic dark red clay. The Somerset levels - a large dairying area - were unique. The low-lying, flat land extended for miles and supported a variety of wetland birds. Huge drainage dykes, known locally as rhynes, surrounded the large fields. Many of the dairy farmers were called Puddy and they all seemed to be related. They were great characters and made me feel welcome, as if I were part of their family.

In the Blackdown Hills the scenery changed dramatically yet again. The fields were very small - anything ranging from half an acre to three acres was not uncommon. High banks faced with local stone (chert - known locally as flints) surrounded them. The banks supported a mixed variety of hedges: beech, holly, ash, oak, hawthorn, blackthorn, willow and, in the valleys, some field maple. These hedges provided a good stock proof barrier, an effective windbreak and a perfect habitat for nesting birds. There were many beech copses on the edges of the

An Irish vet looks back
by Fergus Ferguson ©

escarpments, known locally as "knobs". Hunting birds were common: kestrels, sparrow hawks, buzzards, little owls, tawny owls and barn owls. I was unaware of it at the time, but this enchanting part of the West Country was to play a major part in my life in the future.

Skibbereen

Towards the end of the fortnight, I was summoned to visit a racehorse. I had had very little previous equine experience and was feeling quite nervous. Peter Swift, a small man with a rather pointed nose, always wore a checked peak cap and jodhpurs. Peter was an experienced horseman who held a National Hunt trainer's licence. He loved his horses and was a conscientious professional trainer. Peter had a small yard of approximately twenty horses. The sick horse was called Skibbereen. It was a homebred horse and was the only one he had trained privately. Skibbereen was a twelve-year old 'flea-bitten' grey thoroughbred gelding – a big strong horse standing at 16.3 hands high, with plenty of bone. A real character and very much part of the family, he had won several good National Hunt races. Peter thought that Skibbereen had not been quite right since he had come in from grass two weeks earlier, he had lost weight and his appetite was depressed. Skibbereen was dull, his abdomen was 'tucked up' but his temperature was normal. The mucous membranes of his eye and mouth were very yellow, indicating that he might have jaundice. I was concerned that he might have liver damage.
Antibiotics and multivitamins were given as an interim measure: I had taken some blood samples to try to make a definitive diagnosis. The prognosis was not good. Peter said that Skibbereen was insured. I advised him to telephone the Insurance Company immediately and to confirm the notification in writing. I suggested that, in the circumstances, it would be advisable to summon a second opinion. Peter agreed, he said that in difficult cases like this, Mr Swann frequently called in an Irish veterinary surgeon – a Mr Leeman from Dorset. Later that evening I received a telephone call from Mr Leeman, who agreed to meet me at the stables the following morning.
Mr Leeman, a tall gaunt man with an aquiline nose, was an experienced equine veterinary surgeon. After carefully examining Skibbereen, he also opined that the horse was manifesting signs of liver damage. Not sure that the disease would necessarily respond to treatment, Skibbereen might have to be put down.
Mr Leeman invited me to join him for lunch in the local pub, telling me that he had also graduated from Trinity College, Dublin and had served in the Royal Army Veterinary Corps in Remount depots. I explained that I was becoming increasingly interested in horse practice, he invited me to spend a week with him when I had finished my locum at Netherzoy.
Mr Leeman was a very popular and well-known figure in the local equine community, since he hunted with several of the nearby active hunts: the Quantock stag hounds, the Devon and Somerset staghounds, the Taunton Vale Harriers and his local hunt, the Cattistock. It was during this time with Mr Leeman that I decided that I might like to specialise in

horse practice. However, I felt that I needed some more experience of agricultural practice since I thought it would be a mistake to specialise too soon. I sought his advice. Mr Leeman agreed with me, taking the view that, since horses were luxury animals, in a recession they might have to be sold. He himself, as a young vet, had found that experience gained in calving and lambing cases could be applied to the more difficult and demanding obstetrical cases in the mare. In respect of experience gained, he did not think it would be a good idea to have all one's eggs in one basket.

The Dorset countryside was breathtaking. During the course of our rounds, he pointed out the various landmarks in the practice. I had never heard about or seen the Cerne Abbas giant - the huge, ancient, fertility hill-figure cut out of the chalk downs, complete with erect phallus, his club held at the ready in his right hand. No one knows who carved him or how old he is. It is thought that the figure may have been incised in prehistoric times. Since time immemorial, young couples who wanted to have children would spend the night on the giant's penis in the springtime. The Dorset Downs and chocolate box villages in Thomas Hardy country were a delight to see. The views from the various monuments in the practice, particularly the Wellington monument high on the Blackdown Hills, were spectacular.

Foxworthy

One lunchtime, Mister Leeman kindly permitted me to read the Situations Vacant columns in the back of his copy of the Veterinary Record. A large, old-established practice called Heals (approximately eighteen veterinary surgeons), in the market town of Foxworthy near to Dartmoor, urgently required an assistant. It was principally large animal. Mr

An Irish vet looks back
by Fergus Ferguson ©

Leeman knew them well. In fact, one of the present partners was the
third generation of veterinary surgeons to practise in that area, he
said that it would be ideal. That evening I made contact and joined
them in due course.

Dartmoor Charlie

I lived in a three bedroom detached house. Initially it was very
lonely since I did not know a soul. To remedy the situation, I joined
the local amateur dramatic society that was great fun. The practice
was very old fashioned. A lady, who always wore a long white coat, ran
the dispensary, she knew all the farmers. Many different drenches were
especially prepared to treat a variety of conditions. The favourite
drench in use was the red drench. When the active ingredients had been
mixed together, red litmus was finally added to give the concoction its
vivid colour. When sick adult cattle were attended and treated, the
assistant was expected to supply a red drench. I was never quite sure
what it contained but I soon learned that dispensing it guaranteed
success: not only with the farmers, but also with the veterinary
partners. On return from a case, the question posed by the senior
partner, Colonel Penhalligon, invariably was: 'Did you give her a red
drench, boy?' It was a win win situation. Failure to dispense it, no
matter what else one had done or not done, seemed to infer that one had
not properly attended to the case.

The practice had an extremely efficient network. Radiotelephones were
the state of the art mode of communication. Two girls manned the
control or base unit in the surgery. Each vet had a handset in his car
and we were all given a contact name. Mine was Dartmoor Charlie.
Individual colours were allocated to each vet. Little coloured pins
were placed in a large ordnance map of the practice located on the
surgery wall. The map had a cork backing to enable the girls to push
the coloured markers securely into the map, indicating the farms to be
visited by every vet on each particular day. The girls kept a lists of
farms which the vets were scheduled to visit. Anyone could see at a
glance where the vets were at any given time. When the vets had
completed a call they reported this to the control unit in the surgery.
In the event of an emergency, the nearest available vet could quickly
be despatched to deal with it. This speedy system was very reassuring
to both the vets and the farmers alike. On one particular day,
unbeknown to the girls, the switch on the control unit became jammed
and the girls' entire conversation was broadcast over the air to all
the vets' cars. The girls, both farmers' daughters in their prime, had
been discussing the details of last night's date! This was a great
source of merriment; it took some long time for them to live this down.

Gaseous bloat

It is a long tradition in the veterinary profession that students come
to gain experience during the vacation, at the various practices
throughout the country. This is known as 'seeing practice'.
Frequently, each vet is allocated an individual student, sometimes for
a week at a time. My student was in his final year at Bristol
University, he was the most enthusiastic undergraduate I have ever met.
This man's thirst for experience was unquenchable, he never missed an

opportunity. On my first evening on duty he asked me to promise to
contact him during the night, should a call come in. I agreed to do
so. At 2.00am I received a call to visit a large North Devon cow at a
farm on the edge of Dartmoor. It was a serious case of bloat. In this
condition, the rumen (the largest compartment of the four stomachs)
becomes distended with methane gas.
We drove to the farm as quickly as we could. Bertie Baskerville from
Zeal farm was a harem scarem type of a character who rarely seemed to
sleep. As mad as a March hare, he had a notorious reputation. Nearly
always, he telephoned during the night, much to everyone's annoyance.
Farmers are always charged extra for night calls but this certainly did
not deter him. As a young man in his late twenties - a bachelor.
Apparently, a maiden aunt had left him the farm in her will. The cow
was blown up like a balloon, she was in great distress and was grunting
periodically. I told Bertie that the gas would have to be released
straightaway. The cow's head was secured with a rope halter and the
shank tied, with a quick release knot, to a metal ring bolted into a
wall. Bertie was a strapping lad and knew precisely how to restrain
his cow, he quickly bent her neck at right angles to her body. This
was achieved by holding her left horn in his right hand and squeezed
her nose using the index finger and thumb of his left hand. With the
cow safely secured by Bertie's sturdy arms, I promptly plunged the
trocar and cannula into the rumen. Once I was satisfied it was in the
right place, I removed the trocar from the rumen. Immediately, a large
volume of gas emerged from the cow's stomach via the cannula. The
relief was instantaneous and dramatic. The trocar and cannula is an
ingenious metal instrument. The trocar is a long pointed instrument
with a handle. The cannula is a tubular hollow instrument made to
receive the trocar. The trocar is placed inside the cannula and they
are both inserted into the stomach at the same time. The pointed
trocar is then removed (like pulling a cork from a bottle) thereby
enabling the gas to escape via the cannula. The cannula is usually
stitched to the cow's skin and left in situ until the condition has
settled. The gas does not emerge from the cow's stomach all at once
but tends to come out periodically every time the stomach contracts.
Bertie suddenly announced he had heard a rumour that the gas was
flammable and it was possible to ignite it. The student nodded his
head in agreement. Bertie wanted to strike a match to see if it would
work. The student readily warmed to Bertie's idea. For my part, I
said that I had done my bit and I wanted no part of it. I positively
advised against it. However, Bertie produced a box of matches from his
pocket. There was no stopping him. I cautioned him again, saying that
if he wished to risk burning the building to the ground (I could see
the hayloft above the loose box), on his own head be it. Bertie struck
a match and the gas ignited, much to the student's delight - they were
definitely two of a kind. One was egging the other on. A small blue
flame appeared about two inches from the cow's hide, rather like the
flame from a Bunsen burner. It increased in size every time the cow's
stomach contracted. I was relieved to see that there was no real
danger. The cow was not harmed in any way.

Interestingly, this was the same gas that I had seen in the bog meadow
at Ballybogillbo. Every veterinary student knows that miners carried
caged canaries down into the mineshafts as a precaution against
explosions from fire damp. Canaries are very sensitive to poisoning by
carbon monoxide. This gas is difficult to detect in the atmosphere
since it is odourless, colourless and tasteless. Miners know that if
the canary dies, it is a warning to them that firedamp is present in
the atmosphere. They must vacate the mine immediately, if they are to
avoid the risk of death or serious injury from an explosion.

The Padstow 'Obby 'Oss

The practice was rapidly expanding. The partners planned to employ an
extra assistant. I was asked if I would be willing to share the
practice house with him, I agreed. The new assistant was called
Douglas Death - pronounced 'Death.' Douglas was quite emphatic that he
should be addressed in the correct way and not by the more common
surname of De'ath. The partners also asked me if I would be willing to
introduce him to the clients. Introductions proved to be a problem:
'This is my colleague, the new vet, Mr Death.' The news went down like
a lead balloon with the farmers. However, he proved to be a very
competent veterinary surgeon and the initial worries about his unusual
name were soon forgotten.

Sharing the house worked very well. There were two teams on the duty
roster, working every other night. Douglas Death and I were on
opposite teams. We took it in turn to cook the evening meal. This
meant that we did not have to work on an empty stomach whilst on duty.
The standard of cuisine was not very high, but we did not starve.
Douglas asked me if it was agreeable that a young lady came to visit us
for a short holiday towards the end of April. This was fine with me.
Jane arrived in due course.

Douglas had heard about the celebrations that take place annually on
May Day at nearby Padstow in Cornwall. I was invited to accompany
them. I agreed. The festivities started early in the morning. Two
'Obby 'Osses began to tour the town separately, each with their own
team of accompanying dancers. A 'Teaser' leads each horse, carrying a
club or baton. The 'Oss is a boat-shaped frame covered with a black
oilcloth with a head painted on it, traditionally in red and white. He
chases the girls who, if caught by him and covered by his "skirt",
will, depending on the girl's marital status, have a baby or find a
husband. This is a very ancient pagan fertility ceremony that is re-
enacted every year, never ceasing to appeal to people's basic needs and
instincts.

The NDNC

One glorious spring day I was summoned to see a lame cow at an isolated
farm near the north Devon coast. I received the name, Gidleigh farm,
together with the map reference, over the radiotelephone. I could see
from the ordnance survey map that the farm was fairly isolated,
situated down a long lane. As I approached the end of the lane that
led to Gidleigh, I noticed a prominent sign that boldly stated NDNC,
with an arrow pointing towards the farm. I wondered what the initials

signified. A hirsute man, tall with a long unkempt black beard,
appeared from the depths of a stone barn. I assumed, correctly as it
so happened, that he must be the resident stockman. When I had
finished attending to the lame cow, I enquired of my assistant: 'I'm
puzzled. Can you enlighten me please? What do the initials NDNC stand
for?'

My query suddenly brought a wide grin to his face, as he replied, 'I'm
surprised that the other vets haven't told you. They are usually
queuing up to visit, especially in the warmer weather, when all the
members are here. The initials stand for the North Devon Nudist Club.
They are a very active group and come from as far afield as Bristol,
Gloucester and London. There isn't much to see at this time of year
but in the summer when everyone is here, it was very hard to
concentrate on milking the cows! Two lovely ladies clad only in green
wellies, pay me a visit early each morning to collect their breakfast
milk fresh from the parlour. When the club bought the farm a few years
ago, I could scarcely believe my eyes, but now vetinree, believe it or
not, I hardly notice them!'

'Sorry ma'am, I didn't see your face!'

A short time later a letter arrived from my mother in Ireland, saying
that she would like to visit me. In two shakes of a lamb's tail, I was
escorting her into my motor car at the nearby Exeter airport. All her
life my mother has been the life and soul of the party - a prima donna,
with an impish sense of fun. Mother has always been vivacious,
garrulous and gregarious, even more so when she had had a few drinks.
Being a farmer's daughter, she loved the countryside and country
people. On the return journey I received a call over the
radiotelephone, requesting me to visit a sick animal on Dartmoor.
It was twilight or what is known in many parts of Devon as "dimpsy". I
attended to the moorland animal – an enormous south Devon cow with
mastitis - in the shippon. Mr. Boskinney followed me back to the boot
of my car. I busied myself dispensing the necessary intramammary
tubes, whilst he stood on my left, attentively listening to my
instructions. My mother, as was her wont, did not wish to miss out on
any farming fun, she wound down the front passenger window.
Glancing at the back of mother's head, the farmer exclaimed, 'I sees
'ee have brought your maid with ye, vetineree.'

This was the cue that mother needed to make her "entrance". Turned her
head and engaged the farmer with a charming smile.

Seeing mother's face, the farmer's brown craggy countenance suddenly
turned a delicate shade of crimson. Somewhat perplexed, having
expected to see the visage of a much younger woman, he raised his cap
and blurted out uncomfortably, 'Oh, I beg your pardon Ma'am, I didn't
see your face!'

An Irish vet looks back
by Fergus Ferguson ©

Winterbourne Monachorum

By now I had experienced most of the routine conditions encountered in
farm animal practice. It was time to move on. I wanted to gain more
equine experience with a view to specialising in horses. In the mid
sixties there were very few equine practices in the country. Those
that did advertise for an assistant were usually inundated with
replies. That week, two posts caught my attention in the Veterinary
Record: one in a specialist horse practice in Newmarket, Suffolk; the
other for an equine and small animal assistant in Winterbourne
Monachorum in the south of England. The Newmarket practice was highly
specialised - much too high powered for me. The thoroughbred race
horses and brood mares were extremely valuable. The countryside around
Newmarket was very flat. It was ideally suited for gallops and
training racehorses - not at all like the rolling hills of Ireland.
Following the interview at Newmarket, I told one of the partners that I
did not think that I had sufficient experience for the post. However,
I was also aware that the vast open skies of East Anglia made me feel
agoraphobic.

A short time later I was offered an interview in Winterbourne
Monachorum in Wiltshire. It was a large, old-established practice
split into three sections: farm animal, equine and small animal.
Several of the partners had served in the Royal Army Veterinary Corps.
A Major Crawshaw, who had been working with horses overseas, had
recently joined the partnership with a view to expanding the equine
side of the practice.

I understood that there had been several applicants for the job. Many
factors worked in my favour. I had seen practice as a student in
Lambourn (one of the principal breeding and training centres) in
Berkshire and the partners knew that practice. They also knew Mr
Leeman from Dorset - they had been in the Royal Army Veterinary Corps
together. Eventually, they offered me the job that, in due course, I
accepted. When I became better acquainted with the partners, one of
them told me that they had interviewed so many graduates they could not
remember who was who. No one had made notes. I always took a pride in
my personal appearance. I had spent some time polishing my brown
leather shoes before the interview. The traditional "spit and polish"
approach had been used. One of the partners had noticed my brogues.
When they came to make a decision, he pointed out to them that not only
were my brogues polished on the toes, but, as I walked out of the door
of the surgery, he noticed that the heels also were shiny. When he
mentioned this fact all the other partners suddenly remembered my
shoes, but none of them could recall my name. It was on the basis of
my polished brogues that I was offered the job. Not only had the
partners noticed them but they always consulted the yardman in respect
of any major decisions to be taken in the practice. I had been having
a chat with him just before I went into the interview and apparently he
had also noticed my highly polished shoes, and he had told them that

68

any man who took a pride in polishing his shoes would also take a pride in his work. This was it! The partners never overlooked the yardman's decision. I had been given the official seal of approval - straight from the horse's mouth.

I knew that Jane lived somewhere near Winterbourne Monachorum. It was here that I met Jane again, who was later to become my wife.

Whiskey and eggs

Initially, Major Crawshaw took me around the practice and introduced me to all the horse clients, he was very keen on racing and knew every horse's pedigree. Major Crawshaw owned a thoroughbred stallion that stood at stud locally, he also owned several thoroughbred brood mares. An excellent surgeon, Major Crawshaw taught me more about horses, in my entire career, than anyone else - he became my mentor. One of my duties was to anaesthetise horses and assist with operations. Major Crawshaw was very much the old school horse vet and, in many ways, quite eccentric, he practised the art of veterinary medicine as well as the science, and he liked to treat horses with colic by administering medicines via stomach tube. Major Crawshaw was a great believer in adding whiskey and eggs to the proprietary colic drink which had previously been made up in the surgery; the whole concoction, when well mixed, was given to horses with colic via the stomach tube. For certain types of colic, a mixture of turpentine and linseed oil was given. In other cases, the stirrup pump was used in conjunction with the stomach tube: Epsom salts was placed in a bucket of water, thoroughly mixed and pumped by the groom.

Major Crawshaw taught me everything I know about passing the stomach tube in horses. I cannot remember ever having seen it demonstrated, or doing it myself, at Trinity. I expect I was playing poker or truant. Initially, he applied the twitch to the horse's muzzle for extra restraint. The groom stood on the horse's right holding the twitch and the rope of the head collar. Major Crawshaw stood on the left side of the horse left. According to the size of the horse, the appropriate sized stomach tube was selected, thoroughly washed and lubricated to reduce friction and facilitate passage. It was then inserted into the horse's left nostril. Just before it approached the pharynx, the groom was instructed to flex the neck. This greatly facilitated the chance of the horse making the essential swallowing movement, as it felt the stomach tube approach its pharynx. As this happened, he would then push the tube further down into the oesophagus or gullet, this being the tube between the pharynx and the stomach. Having previously washed and flattened the hair on the left side of the horse's neck, the distension of the flexible and muscular oesophagus is clearly visible, thus confirming that the stomach tube is in the correct position. If the tube has inadvertently entered the trachea or windpipe nothing will be seen since the trachea is a rigid structure. Major Crawshaw regarded this as the acid test, he also relied on the "feel" of the stomach tube. If it is in the right place, ie in the oesophagus - resistance will be felt. Alternatively, if it is in the wrong place, ie in the trachea - no resistance will be felt. Other colleagues used different tests, but he considered these unreliable. Major Crawshaw always worked very quickly, taking the view that if everything was to hand and ready, it was important to proceed as quickly as possible, particularly in young thoroughbreds, before the horse realised what was happening, warning me that in exceptional cases the oesophagus could be abnormally placed. Very occasionally it can be situated on the right hand side of the horse's neck. If the visibility was poor (on a dull day or at night time), he would use a battery-operated lamp strapped to his forehead, so that he could direct the beam of light onto the horse's neck at the critical time, to enable him to confirm that the stomach tube was in the correct place. Major Crawshaw cautioned me against pouring any medicine down the stomach tube unless I was absolutely certain that it was in the right place. If the stomach tube has inadvertently entered the trachea, any medicine administered or poured down the stomach tube will gravitate straight to the lungs. Such a mishap is potentially fatal. Although Major Crawshaw liked to have everything ready and to proceed as fast as possible, he counselled against removing the stomach tube too quickly, since this might precipitate a nose bleed.

After a while, when I had gained more experience, Major Crawshaw decided to turn me loose on the horse owning public. On my first night on duty on my own, I had to visit a hunter mare with colic owned by a Lady Ffrench-Fetherstonhaugh, living in a beautiful manor house in one of the nearby chalk valleys. As I drove into the cobbled courtyard, I could see Lady Ffrench-Fetherstonhaugh and the groom standing beside the horse in the old-fashioned cage-boxes, anxiously awaiting my arrival. The groom was frantically trying to stop the mare (a medium size dapple-grey) from rolling. Lady Ffrench-Fetherstonhaugh was holding a bottle of Irish whiskey in one hand and a jug containing two fresh eggs and an egg whisk in the other. Her ladyship broke the two eggs into the jug and poured in a liberal quantity of Irish whiskey. I added the practice colic drink and the whole was beaten together with the whisk. I then administered this concoction by stomach tube. Everything had gone according to plan. Major Crawshaw's words of wisdom had held me in good stead. The medicine successfully administered, an antispasmodic and pain-relieving injection was given into the jugular vein, to relieve the spasm of the intestine and to lessen the pain.

Lady Ffrench-Fetherstonhaugh invited me into the Manor House for a drink, showing me the butler's sink and invited me to wash my hands. Understandably, I was feeling quite nervous. It was the first case of colic that I had dealt with alone. Hitherto, I had never actually passed the stomach tube. I was still thinking about the case as I washed my hands. Then I wondered why Lady Ffrench-Fetherstonhaugh was staring at me, askance. It suddenly dawned on me that, in my nervous state, I had moved to one side of the sink, grabbed the beautiful lined curtain and was busily drying my hands on it - instead of the adjacent roller towel.

Scabies

My time was spent between equine and small-animal duties. One evening, a mongrel dog with a chronic skin condition, was presented to me. This

An Irish vet looks back
by Fergus Ferguson ©

was obviously causing its owner, a Mr Smith, a great deal of anxiety.
Scamp was covered in sores, since he had been constantly scratching
himself for some long time. I suspected that it might be sarcoptic
mange: a parasitic disease, where the microscopic mite lives under the
skin and reproduces at an alarming rate. It is a minute oval-shaped
mite possessing four pairs of legs. This fiendish little devil is just
visible to the naked eye. I took a skin scraping and left Mr Smith and
Scamp with the nurse while I conveyed the sample next door to the
practice laboratory for analysis. Potassium hydroxide was applied to
the skin scraping and, once the microscope was in focus, I could see
several sarcoptic mange mites crawling around in the solution.
Reference to the practice parasitology textbook confirmed that it was
indeed the dreaded sarcoptic mange. Apart from causing a dog great
distress, the significance of this particular parasite is that
occasionally it can spread to human beings who have direct contact with
the animal. If this happens, it causes skin lesions, with associated
severe irritation, and is known in human medicine as scabies.
When I returned to the consulting room, I told Mr Smith that the
diagnosis was indeed sarcoptic mange and prescribed a lotion to be
applied periodically to Scamp's skin. In those days, a foul-smelling
preparation called Benzyl Benzoate was used. When a veterinary surgeon
is presented with what is termed a zoonosis, that is to say, a disease
of animals that can be transmitted to man, he is duty bound to make
further enquiries.
'Mr Smith, are you aware that this parasite can be transferred to human
beings? It causes a condition called scabies. Are you, or any members
of your family, scratching or affected with skin lesions?'
Shock, horror. This large man, who had been quietly seated throughout
the consultation, leapt up from the chair, ripped off his woollen
jumper and, quick as a flash, unbuttoned his shirt and showed me the
extensive skin lesions across his entire chest, saying with feeling: 'I
have been scratching these for weeks.'
I could see that the young nurse was somewhat taken aback by this
sudden exposure - Mr Smith's chest looked like a piece of raw meat. 'Is
anyone else in your family similarly affected?' I persisted.
Before I had a chance to do or say anything further, or elicit a
response from him, he turned on his heel and made for the consulting
room door, which led directly to the Waiting Room. He thrust open the
door and to the utter amazement of the packed waiting room - there was
standing room only - he shouted to his wife: 'Oi, Maisie, the vet wants
to have a look at you.'
His wife, a small lady, about five feet one inches tall, shuffled
nervously into the consulting room, conscious of everyone's eyes
following her. I rapidly closed the door and quickly reassured the
lady that no examination was necessary. Her husband then informed me
that his wife's condition was similar to his - but much worse. As
grandparents, they had several children and innumerable grandchildren
living in and around the town, who visited them regularly, who all
loved Scamp and had frequent contact with him, when they came to visit.
It then transpired that the entire family was similarly afflicted, they

An Irish vet looks back
by Fergus Ferguson ©

all had skin lesions and they were scratching violently. Most of them
had visited their respective doctors. Some had been to see skin
specialists and some were waiting to see consultants. As far as I
could ascertain none of the doctors had made a definitive diagnosis.
I felt duty bound to contact the attending doctors - I had the benefit
of having seen the horrid sarcoptic mange mite under the microscope and
knew what I was dealing with. I also knew that the causes of many skin
conditions in man are obscure and are notoriously difficult to
diagnose. I enquired from Mr and Mrs Smith whether they had any
objections to my contacting the various doctors involved. All
veterinary surgeons are under a duty of confidentiality and, generally
speaking, they cannot divulge any information appertaining to their
clients or their animals without the owner's consent. Both agreed to
my request.
In due course they supplied me with a list of all the doctors,
dermatologists and consultants involved in the care of the individual
members of their families. I contacted the various doctors concerned.
The reception was very mixed. I discovered that they had made all
sorts of diagnoses and tentative diagnoses, but no one had actually
diagnosed scabies. One older doctor, who had been treating Mrs Smith's
skin lesions for some time, was extremely grateful and relieved to
receive my call. 'What did you give the dog?' he enquired.
'Benzyl Benzoate solution,' I replied.
'Oh, the old Benz Benz!' he exclaimed. 'Do you think it would work on
Mrs Smith?'
The Flymo accident
A retired brigadier had recently heard about the invention of the Flymo
grass cutter, with a small orchard adjacent to his home he had wanted
to keep the grass trimmed. In due course, he purchased a Flymo but
needed a substantial extension cable since there was no electrical
three pin socket near the Orchard. His neighbour's horse was grazing
beside his orchard. Plugging the extension cable into a socket he
dangled it over a post and rail fence and started cutting the grass
with his new toy. After a while, when the brigadier had almost finished
mowing the grass, there was a sudden bang and the machine abruptly
stopped working. Looking around and to his horror, he saw his
neighbour's horse stretched out on the ground. The poor animal was
making brave attempts to stand up but was unable to do so. The local
vet was telephoned who visited forthwith. On careful examination, he
was of the opinion that the horse had broken its back since he could
see that it had chewed right through the extension cable where it had
been dangling over the post and rail fence. When the vet arrived, he
was of the opinion that the horse had been electrocuted. It was shod on
all four feet. The vet thought that the electricity had earthed through
the metal shoes and this had made the horse's spine go into violent
spasms. The vet said that the horse would have to be destroyed since it
was not possible to treat a broken back, but advised that, in the
unusual circumstances, they should seek a second opinion. This was good
professional advice since a case of this nature has many ramifications.

An Irish vet looks back
by Fergus Ferguson ©

Was the horse insured? Was the brigadier covered by insurance for third-party liability? This is just a couple of relevant questions that the incident raised.

When I arrived at the scene of the accident, the brigadier was understandably extremely distressed. It hadn't occurred to him that a horse might chew through an electric extension cable and expose the interior electrical wires. Horses are curious animals and will frequently chew post and rail fences, the top edge of a half door of a loose box and any other obstacle that is within their reach. Horses are quite sensitive to shock by electricity. The horse was trying to raise itself by using its front legs but both hind legs and tail were flaccid and immobile. It was very upsetting to watch its futile attempts to raise itself. I said to the brigadier that the attending veterinary surgeon had made a correct decision and that the horse would have to be put out of its misery forthwith. Further investigations such as insurance cover and any other niceties would all have to be sorted out later. I loaded a single bullet into my small handheld pistol and shot the distressed animal. It is strange to relate that many of the veterinary textbooks recommend that the vet should draw two imaginary lines from the base of each ear to the opposite eye; where these notional lines intersect, is the correct place to shoot a horse. Major Crawshaw had cautioned me about this since he claimed that frequently one book copied another and somehow this erroneous information had entered veterinary literature. The proper place to shoot a horse was 2 inches below the nuchal crest and that this precise position is very easy to locate. The nuchal crest is the ridge of bone at the top of the horse's skull where the forelock is attached. I was assured that I would know from my knowledge of equine anatomy that the horse's brain was directly under this point. Furthermore, if I had followed the advice tendered by many of the equine textbooks, the bullet would enter the frontal sinuses. This would instantly stun the horse (causing it to collapse immediately) but would not kill it, since to properly perform euthanasia in a horse, a bullet would have to go directly into the horse's brain. I have followed major Crawshaw's words of wisdom on every occasions and have never had any difficulty with euthanasia in the horse.

The drainpipe disaster

One early autumn afternoon, major Crawshaw had left a message on the diary to rasp a horse's teeth at a large estate in one of the many chalk valleys outside Winterbourne Monachorum. His name is Samson, the message stated. I was detailed to meet the estate manager at 3 PM sharp. As I drove into the large yard, the estate manager was standing on the large expanse of concrete in the middle of the rectangular. My patient was standing secured to a metal downpipe. Samson was a large substantial dark brown gelding about 16 three hands high at the withers, wearing a leather head collar and the lead rein that was ominously tied to the downpipe. I introduced myself as the new vet from Winterbourne Monachorum and that I had come to rasp Samson's teeth. The estate manager was a tall, well-built man with a mass of black, curly hair and was wearing beige smock coat, together with black Wellington boots. He did not seem to be familiar with horses but looked as if he would be more at home handling beef cattle.

I suggested that it might be safer if we brought Samson into one of the many empty stables but the estate manager immediately retorted with much bluster, 'I know exactly what I am doing. I have been to agricultural college and have been handling animals for years. We will do the job here since I have already tied him to the downpipe.' I got the distinct impression that somehow this routine consultation was not going to go to plan. I could see that there were innumerable flies buzzing around and irritating Samson. Samson was becoming quite agitated since he was swishing his tail and stamping his huge front feet. It was the time of year that horses dread especially when horseflies buzz incessantly under their abdomen.

In this type of situation, it is probably unwise to become involved in an altercation, particularly with an older, dogmatic and inflexible busy man. I said, 'It would be prudent not to have Samson tied to this metal downpipe, since once I start to rasp his teeth, he might pull back or rear, particularly with all the flies irritating him.' I could see that all appeals to logic and common sense were to no avail. The estate manager had already adopted an intransigent stance and knew exactly how the job was going to be done. He wasn't going to be told how to do anything, especially when it came from an inexperienced young vet straight out of veterinary College. From previous experience, I have found that if a tentative start is made to do the job and it looks as if it is going to be fraught with danger, the client might see the error in his ways and agree to alter his rigid posture. However, my instincts told me the situation was hopeless.

I slowly and quietly approached Samson, with my tooth rasp in my right hand, but as soon as Samson realised that something was going to happen, he panicked, using his enormous strength to pull on the lead rope that the estate manager had tied to the metal downpipe. Suddenly, the entire cast iron downpipe pulled away from its meagre wall attachments crashing onto the concrete surface below, making an enormously, loud clonking noise in the process. This calamity totally "spooked" Samson, as he did what horses instinctively did in a situation like this and simply pulled harder and harder on his tether. Of course, the cast-iron downpipe was an integral part of the stables drainage system and was attached to the guttering and all the other downpipes in the yard. They, too, came crashing down onto the unforgiving concrete below with a resounding clatter. The sudden movement and excessive noise created by the falling cast-iron metal drainage system made Samson bolt across the yard, pulling the whole caboodle behind him. The more he pulled, the more noise the metal cast-iron made on the concrete which only frightened him more. Samson could see that his only means of escape was to gallop straight through the open gate situated at the end of the yard into the green field beyond. Since my professional advice had been treated with contempt, and everything had gone awry, I thought the best thing for me to do in the circumstances, was to keep my counsel and vacate the premises as soon as possible.

An Irish vet looks back
by Fergus Ferguson ©

Carbon monoxide poisoning in a dog, a cat and a budgerigar.
I received an emergency call to visit three individual pets that were
owned by an elderly lady.
When I arrived, the lady explained that she had been feeling unwell for
some time and upon returning from shopping, the cat and the budgerigar
were dead. "Winston", the large Great Dane dog, also looked unwell. It
suddenly occurred to me that this could be some sort of poisoning,
either in the air or in the drinking water. I quickly eliminated the
possibility of contaminated water and wondered what toxic substance
could be airborne. My attention focused on an antiquated gas-fired
range and I wondered if this could be a case of carbon monoxide
poisoning. Since I thought that the owner could also be at risk, I
suggested that we should go outside with the dog since I felt that we
could discuss the situation without being at risk. Carbon monoxide gas
is a colourless, odourless and tasteless poison that has an insidious
effect on all living creatures. I telephoned the Gas Authority, briefly
explain the circumstances and requested an urgent visit. In due course,
a representative from the Gas Board appeared and confirmed my
suspicion.
The replacement budgerigar
This was potentially a very sad case. A middle-aged lady, who lived
alone, frequently brought her budgerigar "Charlie" to the surgery to
have its nails clipped. The lady was well-dressed, with a matter-of-
fact disposition. Hitherto, I had never clipped a budgerigar's nails or
beak and was feeling somewhat apprehensive. I managed to extricate the
budgerigar from its cage with considerable difficulty with my left hand
(taking great care not to damage its wings) and held it securely, but
not too tightly, to enable me to clip its toenails. I had placed the
metal clippers in my right hand and had started to clip the
budgerigar's toenails when it suddenly collapsed and died. So far as I
was concerned, this was totally unexpected. I could see from the
practice card index that this clipping of the nails was a routine
procedure and had been performed regularly for several years. I was
fearful that I might have caused the problem. I thought it best to seek
a second opinion so I excused myself, left the consulting room, with
the client and the practice nurse, and went into the private part of
the premises to see if any of the vets were available. The senior
partner was there but he normally attends to farm animals.
Nevertheless, I explained what had happened and he enquired if I had
warned the client about the risks of a heart attack during the
procedure. I stated that I had not done so since I was not aware that
there was such a risk. The senior partner was quite philosophical about
this and informed me that this was normal practice. He suggested that I
might take some money from the petty cash tin, go along to the pet shop
around the corner and purchase a replacement budgerigar. I did this
straightaway. On arriving at the local pet shop, I asked if I could
purchase a young male budgerigar. The owner said certainly and placed
the young budgerigar in the proffered practice metal cage. On returning
to the consulting room, the budgerigar was lying on the table as dead
as a door nail. I tendered my apologies to the client and said how

sorry I was that this had happened, but that I had purchased a budgerigar from the nearby pet shop as a possible replacement. I knew that the lady lived alone and might be very lonely without a budgerigar to talk to. I did not know what the outcome was going to be but thought that I had nothing to lose. To my delight and relief, the client was very understanding and said that it was extremely kind of me to purchase another budgerigar as a replacement for "Charlie". The lady warmed to the idea and to my relief, she said that "Charlie" must be getting to the end of his days and that she had been thinking recently how old he was and that he wasn't going to last forever. Without saying a word, I removed the replacement budgerigar from the metal practice basket and place the new budgerigar in the owner's cage, wishing them well and reassuring the owner that it was a very young male bird and hopefully it would have many happy years in front of it.

The snared cat

It was my turn to do evening surgery. It was exceedingly busy. Towards the end, the secretary said that some clients wanted to bring their cat in as a matter of urgency. The tortoiseshell female cat had been missing for over a week. On its sudden return, the owners noticed a large circular skin lesion that totally surrounded Tiddles abdomen. When I examined Tiddles I could see that there was a severe circular skin lesion right around the abdomen - the smell was nauseating and innumerable maggots were just about to emerge from the depths of the skin. I wondered why the cat had been missing for so long and suggested to the owners that it would be best to admit Tiddles for a general anaesthetic, to try to ascertain the cause of the nasty skin lesion. The owners agreed. Once anaesthetised, it was easier to examine Tiddles since hitherto examining Tiddles was causing her considerable pain. I felt something hard deeply embedded in the skin and realised that it was a metal rabbit snare. This was why Tiddles had been missing for so long since she was probably trying to disentangle herself from the ever tightening wire that must have been secured around her abdomen. A snare is a thin wire noose set to trap animals (such as rabbits or foxes) that some people regard as pests. They are intended to catch the animals around the neck like a lasso. They are indiscriminate in their use and frequently inquisitive cats become trapped by this cruel trap. Sometimes a bait is left to tempt the animal to put its head in the noose.

Once anaesthetised, I had to disentangle the snare with a pair of pliers. When the metal snare was removed from Tiddles skin, I had to clean the grossly contaminated skin to enable me to remove the innumerable maggots that had developed from flies laying their eggs on the smelly skin. Antibiotic ointment was applied all around the affected parts and an injection of penicillin, together with follow-up penicillin capsules and antibiotic puffer powder. It was decided to leave the wound unstitched to allow it to drain.

In four weeks, Tiddles had made a complete and uneventful recovery.

Tidworth polo week

An Irish vet looks back
by Fergus Ferguson ©

One of my duties at Winterbourne Monachorum was to attend a week of
polo at Tidworth in Hampshire. Everything had been proceeding without
drama until one of the ponies (a piebald mare called Poncho) suddenly
collapsed during a chukka. It was lying stretched out on the grass, was
not moving or breathing and ominously a trickle of blood was running
down its forehead from a point where a horse would be shot. I touched
its eyes and it did not blink. There was no pulse palpable under its
mandible and the heart beat could not be detected with the stethoscope.
When I pinched its rectum, there was no response. Poncho was obviously
dead. There was nothing for me to do except to try to ascertain the
cause of the sudden death. Several of the spectators were speculating
that Poncho had been shot by a sniper with a rifle but this notion was
quickly dismissed since no one had heard any gunshots. It was not an
unreasonable suggestion since the small fracture of Poncho's skull was
located precisely where a veterinary surgeon would shoot a horse. I
said that I would have to carry out a post-mortem before I could be of
any further help. Arrangements were made for the removal of Poncho, as
quickly as possible, since the chukkas could not continue with a dead
polo pony lying on the grass.

The next day, on my way to the Polo competition, I called in at the
local hunt kennels. A discreet, circular hole, about the size of the
tip of a man's index finger, was present just above Poncho's brain.
There was no sign of a bullet. However, what was patently obvious from
the post-mortem examination that Poncho had an abnormally thin cranium
just above the brain. During chukkas, polo ponies quite often have
their heads near the ground, particularly if they are making a sudden
turn. I thought that Poncho had possibly been inadvertently hit on the
head by either the hard, plastic ball but more probably from a mallet
or stick.

The poker school

A short time after I arrived in the practice, a poker school commenced.
The vets would play about every three months. We took turns to host
the sessions. The games continued into the small hours. The stakes
were never very high but the fun was good.

We always tried to have at least five vets to play, since this made it
more exciting. The mathematicians, tacticians, gamblers and bluffers
were soon discovered. It engendered a spirit of camaraderie amongst
the vets.

Highland Wedding

A great buzz developed in the practice. A local national hunt steeple
chaser trained by GB (Toby) Balding at Weyhill in Hampshire was running
in the Grand National. Many local punters, including the vets, thought
that he might have a chance of winning. So far as I can recall,
Highland Wedding was a twelve-year-old and it was unusual for an older
horse to win the big race. He won. All the vets had backed him, at
long odds, some time before the race. There were great celebrations,
not only in the practice but also amongst the stable lads, when the now
famous horse returned to his stables in the small hamlet of Weyhill.
The nearby pub at Fyfield was renamed "Highland Wedding" in his honour.

An Irish vet looks back
by Fergus Ferguson ©

The Romany Gypsies

Major Crawshaw castrated the expensive thoroughbred colts and left the rest for my attention. This experience was invaluable. Colts are normally castrated in one of two ways: the operation is either performed with the colt unconscious under a general anaesthetic or with the colt fully conscious using a tranquilliser and local anaesthetic injected into the testicles. If the latter procedure is adopted the colt remains standing. This approach is generally referred to as castrating a colt "standing". The former procedure was adopted for nervous or unbroken colts, or where the owners were inexperienced in handling horses or were frightened of them. Provided they were halter-broken, I preferred to castrate the colts standing.

Sometimes gypsies owned them. These were genuine Romany gypsies who lived in horse-drawn caravans, temporarily parked in one of the many green lanes in the area. The gypsies always insisted on paying cash in advance. This made me very uneasy since I preferred to complete the job first. However, they were adamant. The colts were usually piebald or skewbald. Frequently they were unbroken. Sometimes they were running free and had to be caught. The pole piece of a rope halter was looped twice through a long straight stick and then dangled in front of the colt's head, rather like holding a fishing rod. The colt was then driven along a wall or a hedge, into the rope halter, and his head secured. At this stage an unbroken colt will try to bolt. To avoid an escape, a lunge line, previously attached to the shank of the rope halter and tied with a quick release knot, could be used as an anchor. Fortunately there were usually many willing hands available for the task. If one were lucky, there might be a tree or post nearby; the colt could be driven round and round until the rope became shorter and shorter. With the colt "at the end of its tether", it was then possible to administer a general anaesthetic by rapidly injecting a barbiturate solution into his jugular vein. The anaesthetic took effect very quickly, usually in a matter of seconds. At this stage in the procedure, the quick release knot came into its own. If this were not so, the colt would be anaesthetised with its head attached to a halter secured halfway up the trunk of a tree or post.

Donovan's dilemma

I was quite friendly with a doctor and his wife who lived and practised nearby. They enjoyed all types of riding and hunting. We had an amicable professional arrangement. If one of their horses were unwell, I would make the initial diagnosis, leaving some follow-up antibiotic injections for them to administer on subsequent days. At the end of the hunting season they telephoned me to say that they were going to the West Indies for a short holiday. The horses had been turned out to grass and were left in the care of their housekeeper - a Mrs Donovan. She was not a horsewoman. Mrs Donovan had had no experience of horses and was terrified of them. One Sunday morning she rang in a dreadful panic asking me to come immediately, saying that one of the horses, Tipperary, an Irish gelding, had gone down with colic. It was a beautiful sunny morning, one of the first days of spring. I said that I could come straight away. However, I enquired from Mrs Donovan if

she would be willing to do a simple test for me before I set forth.
She agreed. I asked her to leave the telephone off the hook, assuring
her I would hang on until she returned.

'Mrs Donovan, fetch an empty bucket and place some horse nuts in it.
Go to the gate, call Tipperary and rattle the bucket. Let me know what
happens.' I waited patiently with the telephone in my hand. A short
time later I heard the housekeeper's footsteps approaching the
telephone.

Breathlessly, she gasped: 'Mr Ferguson, I don't quite know how to say
this to you. I called to Tipperary and rattled the bucket of nuts as
you suggested. Standing up, he walked across the field to the gate
where I was standing and ate every last nut in the bucket. He now
seems to have made a complete recovery!' I felt certain that the horse
had been lying fast asleep, enjoying the first blink of early spring
sunshine.

The Hobday operation

Major Crawshaw was an acknowledged expert on the Hobday operation in
horses. This procedure derives its name from the late Professor Sir
Frederick Hobday, a professor of veterinary surgery, who performed
large numbers of these laryngeal ventriculectomies in horses. Sir
Frederick and the technique became so well known that eventually to
Hobday a horse became part of the English language.

Sir Frederick was the ninth principle of the Royal Veterinary College
(RVC), in London.

In larger horses, usually 16.2 or 16.3 hands high or over, a condition
known as whistling or roaring frequently develops. This is a
hereditary condition and a paralysis of the left recurrent laryngeal
nerve ensues. In turn this causes a wasting of the muscles of the left
side of the horse's larynx. Consequently, the horse makes an
inspiratory noise at the canter due to interference with the movement
of air - hence the name, whistling or roaring. This abnormality is
thought to interfere with the horse's ability to perform, thereby
slowing the horse, particularly when galloping at speed.

Major Crawshaw was a very keen sportsman, particularly enjoying a spot
of fishing. Frequently he indulged his passion, taking his family with
him to Ireland. Major Crawshaw had a horsey friend, an Irishman called
Major Charles Ponsonby, who was his Irish connection, as it were. They
met when he was on holiday. Major Ponsonby farmed in Ireland and, as I
recall, had a small thoroughbred stud - about twenty brood mares. Major
Ponsonby was very well known in the horse world in the locality.

Major Ponsonby was well placed for National Hunt racing in the
wintertime since he lived fairly close to both Punchestown and
Leopardstown racecourses. In the summertime he enjoyed showing and
frequently entered his own heavyweight show hunters.

Major Ponsonby would telephone periodically, asking us to come over to
Ireland to perform these Hobday operations. It was always very
difficult to pin him down, as to the precise number of horses that
required surgery. When pushed, he would say things like: 'Ah sure,
there might be one or there might be a dozen!'

An Irish vet looks back
by Fergus Ferguson ©

For a young vet, keen to gain any kind of experience with horses, these trips were always very exciting. As the "boy" it was my job to make sure that we had all the instruments and anaesthetic equipment necessary for the trip. Major Crawshaw referred to these expeditions as "flying surgery". We would turn up at some obscure, isolated hill farm. The horses would appear out of the mist, undergo the operation and disappear again when they had recovered.

Major Crawshaw did not like driving, so I agree to drive. We travelled from Winterbourne Monachorum in Wiltshire to catch the overnight ferry from Fishguard in Wales to Rosslare in Ireland. On our travels to and fro, Major Crawshaw regaled me with stories about his life as a young vet. Apparently, during the war, Major Crawshaw had been in the 8th Army in North Africa, stationed in remount depots where he had hobdayed hundreds of mules. The farrier major oversaw all the preparatory work. The vet could hobday as many mules as he pleased. This was where he had gained all his experience of the Hobday operation. These mules, being pack animals, were then dropped by parachute together with all the supplies, ammunition and guns, behind enemy lines. This greatly assisted the 8th Army with their advance through the Italian hills. Major Crawshaw told me that, once hobdayed, the mules cannot whinny or neigh and therefore could not be detected by the Germans.

The Christmas box

When I arrived in Winterbourne Monachorum the practice had arranged lodgings for me. I stayed with a charming couple, a Mr and Mrs Biggins. They were very kind to me and made me feel a part of the family. Some time before Christmas a large cube-shaped box wrapped in thick brown paper arrived in the post. Addressed to Mr and Mrs Biggins with bold instructions on the outside 'Do not open until Christmas Day.' It definitely looked very like a Christmas present. The Biggins had children and grandchildren living in the vicinity. They kept looking at it every day wondering what it might contain. There was much speculation. I light-heartedly enquired if they would like me to X-ray the box. Eventually their curiosity got the better of them. Asking if I would be willing to take the X-rays. I said that I would, provided the partners agreed. The partners raised no objection. The Biggins were very excited. As agreed, the mysterious box was carefully transported to the surgery and X-rayed.

An X-ray will only reveal opaque substances. We thought, on the balance of probability, that the contents would be radiolucent, and that the investigation would not be very productive. The result took us totally by surprise. It was quite spectacular. Complete in every detail, a set of one dozen glasses was revealed. Individual glasses were inscribed with each family member's name written in radio-opaque paint. More importantly, and worryingly, two of the glasses were shown to be broken. Cracks could clearly be seen on two of the tumblers. The parcel had been sent by REGISTERED POST. Obviously the Biggins would be in a better position to make a claim if they brought the unopened box, together with the supporting X-ray, to the Post Office as evidence that the contents were in fact damaged, prior to the box being opened. So far as I can recall, they made a successful claim. Post Office staff thought that it was very peculiar.

The bullmastiff with heatstroke

It was a searing hot, humid Saturday afternoon at Winterbourne Monachorum and everybody was busy with shopping. I suddenly received an emergency call from the member of the public to say that a dog was locked in a car in the Market Square and they were fearful that it was overheating. I grabbed my veterinary bag and ran as fast as I could to the square. It wasn't too difficult to find the location since a large anxious crowd had gathered around the four-door car. A burly police sergeant had just arrived on the scene and everybody was waiting for the vet to arrive. The dog, a large brindle bullmastiff, had collapsed in the back seat of the motorcar and all the windows were tightly shut. There was no sign of movement from the dog. The owners were nowhere to be seen. I feared the worst so I instructed the police sergeant to open the motorcar. He smashed the window with one stroke of his truncheon, placed his arm through the car window and opened the front door. After leaning into the back seat, he opened the back door to enable me to examine the large dog. It was not moving or breathing. It did not respond when I touch its cornea. I took its temperature and to my horror, it was 103 °. Clearly, the dog was dead due to hyperthermia. The police sergeant and the assembled crowd were horrified. Just as I was giving my opinion to the police sergeant, the family returned from afternoon shopping. They, too, were aghast. The family had left their beloved dog in the car, as they had done so on many times in the past, but never on a hot day. The police sergeant gave them a lecture but since they were already extremely upset by the loss of their treasured dog caused by their negligence, and were clearly contrite, the police sergeant was not mindful to take matters further.

Operation Dapple Grey

Major Crawshaw was asked to organise the team of honorary veterinary surgeons to cover the army three-day event horse trials near Winterbourne Monachorum, he invited me to become a member of the team. I agreed. It was the first time that I had ever acted as honorary veterinary surgeon at an equine event. I was finding this a daunting prospect, since I was aware that during any three-day event there could be major equine disasters.

The army regarded this as a full-scale military operation, referring to it as Operation Dapple Grey the Seventh. In due course, my appointment as honorary veterinary surgeon was confirmed. I received my badge, entry pass and invitation to lunch. Since this was an official military operation and I was part of it. Every day I received reams and reams of "bumph". Most of it was completely irrelevant and was duly filed in the bin! I was scheduled to be on duty for the cross-country day. Written instructions were sent. I was to report at 10.00 hours precisely, at a specified map reference.

I arrived as instructed on the dot of 10.00 hours, at the prearranged spot, in a small copse overlooking parkland. I wondered what would happen next, as I turned off the car engine. There were no further

instructions in the letter. As I climbed out of my motor car, I
noticed two soldiers marching straight towards me. Suddenly they came
to an abrupt halt about a yard in front of me, stamped feet and saluted
rigidly, saying: 'Corporal Jones reporting for duty, Sah.' His
companion was a Lance Corporal, they both remained stock still,
standing rigidly to attention in front of me. I nervously looked over
my shoulder, thinking that they must be saluting someone else. Since
there was no one else in the wood, I realised that it was me they were
saluting. I was unused to army discipline and unsure what I should do.
I felt perhaps that I should say something.
I tentatively enquired of the Corporal: 'I assume that you are both
here to escort me to any injured horses?'
The Corporal replied: 'Sah.'
My confidence was slowly increasing. 'Lead me to your vehicle,' I
said, trying to sound confident.
The Corporal replied, 'Sah,' turned on his heel and led the way to the
army Landrover.
I then transferred all my emergency equipment (including my gun) into
the back of the Landrover. We were in touch by radio with the base
control unit at General Head Quarters. We had a panoramic view of a
large portion of the delightful parkland and were ideally located to
view the cross-country course.
Later in the day the heavens opened - torrential rain. The conditions
rapidly deteriorated - thunder and lightning. The going was becoming
very heavy. Both the competitors and the horses were finding the jumps
much more difficult. I was becoming increasingly apprehensive. Just
in front of the land rover, a young lady rider was collecting her horse
in readiness for the next fence, when there was a terrific flash of
lightning. Both horse and rider collapsed, right in front of our eyes.
I jumped out of the land rover and was at the scene in an instant. The
horse was my responsibility. The dark bay gelding, Drumshambo, with a
wall eye, lay stretched out on the ground. I touched his cornea, he
did not blink nor was he moving or breathing. I could not feel his
pulse or hear his heart with my stethoscope. It was obvious that
Drumshambo was dead. It seemed clear to me that the horse had been
struck by the huge flash of lightning. The doctor arrived to attend to
the young rider, lying unconscious near her horse. I made arrangements
with the army to remove the dead horse from the course. I was
attending to this, when my driver received another emergency call over
the radio from GHQ.
I realised that we would need to use the four-wheel drive. In no time,
they had whisked me to the scene of the accident. Both Cornish horse
and rider had had a very bad fall. Tresillian, the large bay gelding
with a white blaze, was in great pain, standing on three legs. I
carefully examined the injured leg. As I did this, I could hear
definite crepitus or crackling of the bones which made up the shoulder
joint. It was fairly obvious that Tresillian had fractured his humerus
(one of the large long bones of the forelimb) and would have to be put
down. Even though it was pouring with rain, a large crowd was rapidly
gathering, curious to discover the outcome of the accident. Tresillian

82

was very well known. I knew that I would have to shoot Tresillian and was worried about the possibility of a ricochet injuring a bystander. I had never shot a horse before. Two problems loomed large in my mind. First, I needed to gain consent from the owner to put the horse down. Second, it was critically important to clear the area of milling bystanders. It was not going to be an easy matter to shoot Tresillian, since he was constantly moving, due to the severe pain.

Suddenly, like manna from heaven, a Landrover appeared. A Colonel stepped out. I had met him once before when he had asked me to rasp his point-to-point horses' teeth. He said, 'I see you are in a spot of bother here, Ferguson. Do you need some help? May I be of any assistance?'

'Yes, Colonel, this horse has broken his shoulder and will have to be shot. People are swarming around everywhere and I am worried that there might be a ricochet. The entire area will need to be cleared. Can you help, please?'

The Colonel instantly replied: 'Leave it to me, Ferguson.'

Two lorry loads of soldiers were parked nearby. With typical military precision, the Colonel summoned the Sergeant: 'Sergeant, Veterinary Officer Ferguson requires the area to be cleared. This horse has to be shot.'

The Sergeant immediately jumped to attention, raised his giant frame and saluted, saying: 'Sah.'

With an instant "about turn" he roared an order to the soldiers in the nearby 4-ton trucks. 'Come on you lot, get fallen in. On the double. One, two, one, two. Line abreast. Area to be cleared.'

Instantly all the soldiers jumped from the covered trucks and fell in, line abreast. The Sergeant then roared a further command: 'All right you lot, on the order to march, area to the front to be cleared - quick march. Left, right, left, right ...'

As the line of soldiers advanced menacingly on the crowd, with notional fixed bayonets, people immediately began to disperse.

When the area was finally cleared, the Sergeant marched up to the Colonel, came to a halt and saluted. 'Sah. Area cleared.'

The Colonel then turned to me, having discharged his duty by the book, saying: 'Okay, Ferguson. Area cleared. Shoot horse.'

One army groom stepped forward to steady Tresillian's head. Another unbuckled the saddle and slipped it off. The rider, an experienced horsewoman, could see that the humerus was shattered, she knew that nothing could be done and authorised euthanasia. Putting her arms round her beloved horse's neck, she said her last goodbye, she then allowed her mother to wrap a tartan rug tightly round her shoulders and lead her away.

Now that the area was finally cleared, I put Tresillian out of his misery. I was trembling with fear. It was not an easy task for a young veterinary surgeon to shoot a horse for the first time in a public place. I thanked the Colonel for his help.

The Corporal was detailed over the radio to escort me to the marquee for lunch. When we arrived at the army headquarters in the centre of the Operation, there were two enormous marquees side by side, one furnished with a red carpet. The Corporal escorted me into this marquee, where I was welcomed by a Field Marshal and a General. From the red circular badge on my lapel, they could see that I was an honorary veterinary surgeon. The Field Marshal introduced himself and then introduced me to the General, who had heard all the details of the two emergencies on the cross-country and were very relieved that I had dealt with them on behalf of the army. The Field Marshal summoned a wine waiter and offered me a drink. We then sat down at the centre of the top table for lunch, they both insisted that I should sit between them. It was a full "silver service" army lunch and the entire marquee was awash with army bigwigs and their wives. I was fast coming to the conclusion that I was in the wrong marquee - this was for VIP's. I mentioned this to the Field Marshal. He insisted that I should stay, saying that the army could not function without veterinary surgeons to deal with emergencies.

Following a very convivial lunch, I decided it was probably time that I returned to my veterinary duties on the cross-country course. The Field Marshal and the General escorted me to the entrance of the marquee. Each in turn enthusiastically shook me by the hand and thanked me for my help. As the three of us stood at the entrance to the VIP marquee, I could see a bowler-hatted Major Crawshaw emerging from the marquee opposite where he had had his lunch. After the Field Marshal and the General had returned inside, Major Crawshaw asked me how on earth I had managed to be admitted to the VIP marquee. I explained that the Corporal had escorted me to that marquee and that the Field Marshal and General, who were welcoming everyone, would not let me leave.

Let sleeping dogs lie

One Sunday just before lunch I received a call from a Mr Bumble, who lived on a large housing estate, requesting an emergency visit. The worried owner reported that his dog, Brandy, had a fork stuck in its side. The assistants had been instructed, if at all possible, not to visit this housing estate, since the vets rarely received payment. Aware of this ruling, I enquired if he could bring Brandy to the surgery. Mr Bumble said that he did not possess a motor car. I asked him whether he could convey Brandy to the surgery by taxi-cab. Following a pregnant pause, he eventually agreed.

Twenty minutes later, I noticed a very small taxi pull up on the kerbside outside the surgery. The taxi driver burst into the surgery, shouting: 'Where's the vet?' He demanded that I come outside immediately. I peered in the taxi window and saw that there was barely room to swing a cat. A huge St Bernard dog (I could see from the name-tag on its collar that he was indeed Brandy) and its keeper were crammed into the back seat. To my utter amazement, the handle of a large garden fork was protruding from the partially open rear door window - I had imagined that Mr Bumble had been referring to a small fork, as in a piece of cutlery! This explained Mr Bumble's initial hesitation concerning the transport arrangements to the surgery. I wondered how on earth they had managed to squeeze into the taxi. How was I to extricate the poor animal without inflicting further injury?

An Irish vet looks back
by Fergus Ferguson ©

The enormous dog was in considerable pain and in a state of shock.
Judging by the doleful look in Brandy's eyes, he seemed to know
instinctively that he was in a predicament and needed my help.
Eager to avoid the possibility of injury, I said to the owner, a minute
man with a hook-nose, who was wearing a pork pie hat: 'Mr Bumble, you
can see that Brandy is in severe pain and he is extremely frightened.
I will have to give him a painkilling injection before we attempt to
move him. This should make him relax and help to ease his pain. We
must avoid further injury. Firstly, I will have to apply a muzzle.'
In normal circumstances, giving an injured and frightened dog an
injection is a hazardous business, but it is even more so in a confined
space. I climbed into the cramped back seat and, with considerable
difficulty, managed to apply an outsize muzzle to Brandy's nose. The
nurse passed me a tray that held a loaded hypodermic syringe together
with its needle.
Trying to appear confident, I said to the dog: 'don't worry old chap,
we'll have you back together again in one piece in a jiffy.' I
breathed a sigh of relief as I administered the injection without
mishap. The question then arose, how best to deal with the offending
fork. Luckily, by this time my patient was snoring peacefully. I sent
the nurse to fetch the biggest stretcher that the practice possessed.
I turned to Mr Bumble to try to enlist his help with the unenviable
task of transporting his charge into the surgery. I had been so busy
concentrating on Brandy, I had not realised that his master had fainted
- the nurse said that that had happened while she was passing me the
syringe and needle. Fortunately, she was a strapping lass - a farmer's
daughter, used to lifting heavy weights on her father's farm - who was
more than willing to help. Brandy, now a dead weight, somehow had to
be rolled over onto the stretcher. We could not proceed out through
the door, since the fork was firmly wedged in the partially open
window. There was only one thing for me to do. I would have to
clamber over the unconscious owner and the dog, to enable me to wind
down the window. The taxi-driver, anxious about attending to his next
fare, was only too willing to assist. With great difficulty, we
managed to manhandle Brandy together with the offending fork onto the
king-size stretcher and lift him up the steps into the surgery. That
was the easy part. The grunts and gyrations of the three participants,
in lifting the massive dog (he must have weighed well over a
hundredweight) onto the operating table, had to be witnessed to be
believed.
I could not ascertain the case history. The curved outside tine of the
fork had penetrated the skin just behind the shoulder blade and had
travelled its full length under the skin over the rib cage. The tip
had emerged and was protruding menacingly, some seven inches further
along, pointing in the general direction of his tail. Obviously, the
fork would have to be removed. It was impossible to obtain the owner's
consent to a general anaesthetic, since he was still lying unconscious
on the back seat of the taxi. Urgent action was required. I could not
wait for him to recover. My head was spinning. What was I to do?
Such unusual cases were not a part of any veterinary syllabus. I

decided to press on. Should I adopt the orthodox, conservative
approach in releasing the intruding implement, by making a full length
surgical incision through the skin between the two puncture wounds?
Alternatively, the straightforward, intuitive, gung-ho, pulling method
had much to commend it. Yes, I was definitely warming to the latter
idea. There was no time for idle speculation. Instant action was
required. My patient was anaesthetised as quickly as possible with an
extra-large volume of barbiturate given intravenously. As he
dramatically rolled over onto his side under the influence of the
anaesthetic, I could see that his vast frame was perilously close to
falling off the practice operating table. Fortunately for the hapless
Brandy, my two sturdy helpers rushed to the rescue. I suddenly
realised that somehow my oversized canine patient would have to be
safely secured to the cleats at the side of the operating table,
otherwise my two trusty assistants would soon collapse from exhaustion.
Something substantial was urgently required to fulfil the job. Where
were my adaptable foaling ropes?
With Brandy's massive limbs safely fastened to the cleats I decided, as
a further precaution, to anchor his collar. This proved to be a wise
afterthought, since I suddenly became acutely aware that the offending
fork would probably have to be extracted from Brandy's flank by
traction. Once the pulling efforts to remove the fork had commenced,
it was not too difficult to imagine how one might become carried away
with enthusiasm. Without the security of the ties, Brandy might have
been pulled inadvertently along the smooth surface of the surgeon's
table and over its edge, precipitating yet another veterinary crisis!
The shaft and handle of the fork were dangling limply from his side at
an oblique angle. I instinctively grasped the handle with my digging
hand (I have always keen on growing vegetables), stabilised the shaft
with my other hand and placed one foot firmly on the edge of the table.
With a robust but carefully controlled tug, I managed to remove the
troublesome foreign body, without causing further harm.
I decided not to suture the two puncture wounds caused by the
penetrating point of the prong, but to leave them open for drainage.
An antibiotic injection was given, and some follow up tablets
prescribed with directions written on the label of the bottle: "To be
administered by mouth daily for five days". By this time, Brandy had
recovered from the anaesthetic and was fit to go home. The observant
nurse reported that the enigmatic Mr Bumble was regrettably still
comatose on the back seat of the taxi. The cab driver was becoming
increasingly impatient - he had an urgent fare waiting and was keen to
return both of his soporific passengers to their home. The somnolent
Brandy was carefully, but laboriously, replaced on to the back seat of
the taxi beside his sleeping master and the long-suffering driver sped
off.
A week later, a next-door neighbour brought Brandy for the routine
check-up. The colossal mountain dog bounced ebulliently into the
consulting room, greeting me like a long lost friend, with an
enthusiastic wagging of his tufty tail. His prodigious bulk and placid
nature made me realise how very useful he would be in rescuing someone

stranded in the freezing Swiss Alps. Fortunately, he had made a complete and uneventful recovery. Both the wounds on his flank had almost healed. I never did find out the whole story - perhaps it was better not to know - a classical case of: "let sleeping dogs lie."

The horse and the onion

Sometimes routine equine cases are not as they appear. This was the case when I was summoned to a riding school horse with colic. Riley, the seven-year old dun cob gelding, about 15.3 hands high, with a distinctive walleye, had been scraping the ground of his loose box with his front shoe, looking around anxiously at his flank and had been rolling on his back in the straw bedding for several hours. I had been in the tack room of this small suburban livery yard and riding school on several occasions and it was obvious from all the old-fashioned bottles on the shelves that routine proprietary medicines were frequently used. The yard was owned and run by a diminutive horsey lady known to all and sundry as Mrs C. This lady was metaphorically born in the saddle since she had spent her entire life involved with horses. The vet was only summoned when the home-made remedies hadn't worked. This was such a case. I took Riley's temperature, but that was normal. The mucous membranes of both eyes were the usual salmon pink colour. I listened to both flanks with my stethoscope and could hear the normal tinkling sounds. I felt his pulse under his chin and it was strong and regular. These were all reassuring signs. In cases of this nature, I always perform a rectal examination since the vet has to watch out for the dreaded cases of strangulation or twisting of the intestine. This is when a part of the horse's gut rotates on its own axis. I applied some obstetrical lubricant to my extended arm glove, asked the groom to use my Chifney bit to give more restraint during the rectal examination, applied a bandage around the base of Riley's tail and positioned him alongside the loose box wall by the loosebox door, so that I could insert my gloved arm into his rectum in safety. Everything was progressing normally until I felt a soft circular lump about the size of a large orange in his rectum. The vet has to check for such conditions as polyps and various other rare equine disorders. I grasped this soft lump and found that it could be moved around inside the rectum. It did not seem to be attached to the lining of the intestine. Since I was holding it in the palm of my hand, I thought I would pull gently on it to see if it could be exteriorised. The next thing I knew, to my astonishment, I was holding a large onion in my hand, complete with the raffia neatly tied around the base of its leaves. It was the type of large onion that could easily have won first prize as an exhibit at any local village show. Knowing the background to the yard and Mrs C's reputation for home treatment, I thought it best to keep my counsel.

I put the onion to one side and gave the horse an injection of a painkilling and antispasmodic drug into its jugular vein. Having applied my trusty Blackthorn twitch to the horse's muzzle, I passed an appropriate sized stomach tube up the horse's nostril and, once I was assured that the tube was safely in the stomach, I asked one of the grooms to pour a mixture of turpentine and linseed oil into the funnel.

An Irish vet looks back
by Fergus Ferguson ©

What of the mysterious onion? I had never come across a situation like this. However, I noticed an empty wooden box for transporting oranges sitting just outside the door of the loose box, and felt that since Mrs C was nowhere to be seen, and due to her small stature, she probably would have needed to stand on the Orange box to enable her to insert the large onion.

I thought it best not to ask too many questions but gave the grooms a good prognosis and suggested that Riley should be given two days' rest.

A donkey mare with tetanus

I was called to see a ten-year old donkey mare, Kathleen that was kept at livery. Kathleen had become very stiff in her movements and was having great difficulty in eating. About ten months in foal. Kathleen was having problems turning around in the loose box. In fact the muscles in her back had become so rigid, she moved around her loose box like a ship turning in a harbour. Ears were erect, her nostrils were flared and her tail was elevated. Kathleen's expression was anxious, she was constipated. When you tapped the side of her face it caused the nictitating membrane or the third eyelid to flick reflexly across the eye. Her head and neck were extended. Kathleen was extremely reluctant to move, her temperature was normal. Kathleen could not lie down. I felt that she might have lockjaw or tetanus, she had not been vaccinated against tetanus. There was no history of a previous wound or evidence of injury to any part of the body. I administered a large dose of crystalline penicillin by intravenous injection. Tetanus antitoxin was also given. I gave the owner a guarded prognosis. Kathleen was not insured. I had not seen a case of lockjaw in either a horse or a donkey before. I thought I would ask Major Crawshaw to give a second opinion. He agreed with my diagnosis.

I visited Kathleen every day and kept her alive by administering a liquid source of food by stomach tube and an intravenous electrolyte solution. I was worried that she might not be able to give birth. Four weeks later her udders bagged up and wax could be seen on the end of her teats. She was also running milk. The pelvic bones had tilted, consistent with a mare that is on the point of foaling. In view of these signs it was obvious that she was about to foal. Kathleen foaled during the night without assistance. Fortunately the foal - a filly - was born alive. The owners were in attendance during the night but, as instructed, did not interfere. They reported the foal was able to stand unaided in an hour and was sucking from its mother within two hours of birth.

All Equidae - horses, donkeys, zebras, etc - give birth at night. This is an evolutionary adaptation enabling them to escape their principal predators - big cats. Having given birth, the mares and foals have to bond together. The foal then has to stand and suckle from its mother to give it strength to enable it to run with the herd. All of this must have taken place before dawn if the foal is to have a chance of surviving.

After an illness lasting six weeks, Kathleen made a complete recovery. Fortunately the donkey foal also lived and developed normally.

Foot and Mouth Disease

In the sixties there was a major outbreak of Foot and Mouth disease. Unlike the more recent 2001 situation, the earlier epidemic was concentrated in one principal area - the Welsh borders, Shropshire and Cheshire. The practice was not directly affected. However, the indirect affect was considerable. Hunting and racing were abandoned and farmers did not want vets (or anyone else for that matter) to visit their farms for fear of spreading the disease. Small animal work was in its infancy. The practice ground to a standstill. It was obvious to all the vets that radical decisions were necessary. I considered that it was my public duty to go, if necessary, to the affected area and fight the epidemic. The partners wanted me to stay behind to attend to equine emergencies at night and weekends when Major Crawshaw was off duty.

I was relieved to hear that I did not have to go to fight the epidemic. One of the vets from the practice volunteered. The stories were not good. It is not a very pleasant task for a veterinary surgeon to be involved in the mass slaughtering and destruction of animals. The pyres of burning bodies were huge. Smoke lingered for weeks. Foot and Mouth disease is a highly infectious viral disease of cattle, sheep, pigs, goats and certain other animals. It has a very high morbidity rate - ie most animals in a susceptible group are affected, but has a low mortality rate ie only a few affected animals in a susceptible group, die. It can cause huge economic loss to any country.

The pride of lions

One afternoon a secretary at the practice said that a circus, who were living in their winter quarters somewhere in the Cotswolds had requested that I attend to some lions. I did not know the first thing about wild animals, and lions in particular. The secretary informed me that they did not want anyone but me! I thought that perhaps my wife and three children, would like to come along for the visit.

When we arrived, the Lions were in an enclosed ring, surrounded by a high wire fence, with a lion tamer inside it. I introduced myself as the vet from Winterbourne Monachorum. The Lion tamer was a rather gung-ho character, with long black hair tied in a ponytail, he informed me that he would open the entrance to the enclosure immediately so I could have a closer look. I said that it was fine for me to stay on the outside of the enclosure and that I was quite happy to perform the consultation from there. There were a dozen lionesses in the pride and one of them had suddenly become lame. Apparently, the pride had been purchased for export and were scheduled to leave shortly. I could see which lioness was lame and pointed this out to the lion tamer, he agreed that I had selected the correct lioness and again he was more than happy for me to come into the enclosure to make a closer inspection. I stood my ground. I asked if it would be possible to separate the lame lioness from the rest of the pride to enable me to concentrate on the one in question. All the lionesses where walking around the perimeter of the enclosure. Using his whip to great effect, he isolated the lame lioness from the rest of the pride, then deftly

An Irish vet looks back
by Fergus Ferguson ©

pulled a rope on a pulley that lifted a metal door allowing all the
lionesses (with the exception of the lame one) to walk through into
another enclosure. I breathed a sigh of relief. I was now able to
examine a single lame lioness without being distracted. Yet again, the
lion tamer invited me to enter the enclosure and I again declined.
I asked the lion tamer to move the lioness around the periphery of the
cage to enable me to observe her gait. 'When did you first notice this
lameness?' I enquired. The lion tamer responded that it had developed
suddenly during routine exercise a couple of days ago. There was no
history of trauma so I thought that she had probably strained a muscle.
'I will have to give her an intramuscular anti-inflammatory injection.'
The lion tamer was quite happy with my diagnosis and treatment. I
selected an appropriate syringe and needle and sucked 10 ml of the
anti-inflammatory injection into the syringe. I placed everything on a
small metal tray in readiness for the hoped-for injection.

Just then, a Land Rover drew up with four sturdy men on board. The
driver seemed to be the owner or keeper of the establishment saying, 'I
assume that you are the vet from Winterbourne Monachorum.' That is
correct, I replied nervously, explaining briefly my diagnosis and
proposed treatment. You and your men have just arrived in time since I
have to administer an intramuscular injection to this lioness. 'How do
you normally inject the Lions?' I enquired. 'How quick are you with
your hypodermic syringe and needle?' he asked. 'Very quick' I replied,
with increasing confidence. 'If you position yourself just outside the
enclosure, I will ask the lion tamer to bring her around the outside to
where you are positioned, and when he cracks his whip, she will stop
just beside you. This normally makes it possible for us to grab hold of
her tail through the cage wire and pull.' Everybody was familiar with
the routine. In a trice, my patient had stopped immediately opposite
the position where I was standing and happily her tail was conveniently
just inside. The four men grabbed hold of it and pulled as hard as they
could. I ceased my opportunity and injected the solution into the
lioness's muscle as quickly as I could. When the lioness felt the pain,
she instinctively leapt forward but fortunately I just had sufficient
time to administer the drug.
I spoke to the keeper and lion tamer instructing them to rest the
lioness for a week and to let me know how she was getting on. 'I think
she has pulled a muscle and a week's rest, together with the effects of
my intramuscular injection, will hopefully cure the problem.' When we
were out of earshot of the lion tamer, the keeper suddenly exclaimed,
'I hope that he (nodding towards the lion tamer) didn't invite you into
the enclosure?' I nodded. 'He tries to do that with everyone, he loves
his work but gets rather carried away with excitement. Recently, he has
undergone extensive plastic surgery since one lioness attacked him from
behind, pinned him to the ground and all the other lionesses joined in,
he is lucky to be alive.'
When I returned to Winterbourne Monachorum, I discovered that the
circus people had telephoned the wrong veterinary practice. Many years
ago, when they visited Buckland Monacorum, they needed some veterinary

attention for a lion and they telephoned the other veterinary practice in the town. An Irish man, who was doing a locum in the practice, attended and apparently he did a very good job. They resolved that if they ever needed veterinary attention in the future, they would ring the Winterbourne Monachorum practice and ask for the Irish vet.

The keeper telephoned me a week later and was pleased to relate that the lioness was no longer lame and that the pride would be able to be exported in due course. I was thanked for my help.

The mad heifer

It was a routine market day at Winterbourne Monachorum, or it was until a freshly calved heifer escaped and terrorised the local community. Occasionally this happens when a heifer is separated from her calf and she will start to behave like a Spanish fighting bull. Running along all the narrow streets flanked by rows of Victorian terraced houses. Initially, it didn't seem too complicated until she scraped the ground with her front feet and attacked anybody that went anywhere near, it suddenly became a crisis. The police were alerted and blocked either end of this Victorian Avenue with their sturdy vehicles. There was no escape. The heifer reached a state of sheer panic since she had been separated from her calf, there were no other bovines anywhere to be seen since, being a herd animal, they do not like to be isolated. Suddenly she made an abrupt right ankle turn, leapt into the small "postage stamp" size front garden of one of the terraced houses and kept going through a low, sliding sash window smashing all the class. Two elderly ladies were sitting inside by the window, sharing one of their regular coffee mornings when this crazed animal charged through the window, showering them with broken shards of glass. Once inside the small room, the heifer just kept going, jumping over the coffee table and smashing all the delicate china. The two ladies were absolutely petrified and in a state of shock. The heifer then proceeded into the small kitchen to the rear, saw some grass through another low sliding sash window and pushed straight through it to the small enclosed garden to the rear. She couldn't go any further since she was surrounded on three sides by a small wall with a wooden fence above it. The police escorted the two terrified ladies outside to safety. They then summoned a firearms officer who was ordered to take position in an upstairs room and to shoot if there was any further threat. The heifer was shaking her head and scraping the ground in fear, in a clear indication that if anyone went anywhere near her, she would charge straight at them. I was summoned to this dramatic situation. I could see that the police marksman could shoot the heifer with his high velocity rifle but this then begged the question, as to how the carcass was to be removed from the small garden to the rear. It could not be guaranteed that the heifer would be killed instantly but might only be maimed. I knew that there was a small alleyway to the side that led from the rear garden to the street and there might just be sufficient room for the local hunt wagon to extricate her. Nothing was certain. At least, the situation was contained since access to the street was barred by police vehicles. Dart guns for this type of situation had just become available to veterinary surgeons. The user needed training and a licence to use them. Certified veterinary surgeons could only use them. I did not have a conventional hand-held gun with me, but even if I did, I could not get sufficiently close to the frightened animal to dispose of it with any degree of certainty and without compromising my own safety. I thought the best thing to do in the circumstances was for the police, now that they had the situation under control, was to summon a veterinary surgeon who had a dart gun and a licence to use it. Furthermore, I believe the police may not have received instructions from the owner to dispose of the animal. The primary duty of the police is the safety of the public.

Larkhill point-to-point

It was the first race meeting of the season. In severe winter weather, sometimes it is not always possible to exercise racehorses on the roads due to snow and black ice. Consequently, horses are not always as fit as they should be. I was on duty as an honorary veterinary surgeon. The final race had arrived without incident. However, on the last race of the day, an extremely large number of horses were "under starter's orders." Suddenly, after one of the most distant jumps had been negotiated, the yellow flag was raised which means that the services of the vet was required. My driver drove across country as quickly as the Army Land Rover would take him. The scene that greeted me was like a movie cavalry charge. Five horses were flat-out on the ground. Before I did anything, I asked the fence judge to divert the race horses away from the fence in question, since I knew that they would be coming around a second time prior to completing the race. Frequently, in these situations, many Job's comforters tender advice to the veterinary surgeon as to what should be done or shouldn't be done. This was one of those situations. One officious busybody pronounced nonchalantly as he passed by, "I hope you have brought your gun with you vet since there are five horses here that need to be shot!" In these situations it is always best to say nothing and carry on with your professional duties. All five horses were lying on their flanks. Some were trying to raise themselves and somewhere just quietly lying still. I knew that there was no immediate hurry to make a decision as the fence judges had diverted the jump in question so that all the horses travelling at speed the next time around could safely pass by on the outside. I instinctively knew that I should play for time since, once the horses had passed the fence the second time, I would be able to examine the horses without distraction. I busied myself getting my equipment from the Army Land Rover, but in reality I was just practising the art of veterinary medicine known as masterly inactivity. When the large field came thundering past (bypassing the fence in question), knowing that this was the last race of the day, I could apply myself to the job in hand without the fear that racehorses travelling at speed might suddenly land on top of me or the fallen horses. I checked all five fallen horses - they were all breathing and were alive. However, one poor horse was showing alarming symptoms. He did not reflexively constrict his rectum when I pinched it, his tail was flaccid and he was unable to move his hind legs. There was no need to do anything for the present so I left him quietly lying on the grass whilst I turned my attention to the other four fallen horses. Happily, they all had strong rectal reflexes, their tails were not flaccid and there was some movement in their hind legs. Since it was the first race of the season, I was hoping that these four horses might be "winded." If so, there was no immediate hurry to do anything. However, when sufficient time had passed, I secured a lunge line around the lower pastern joint and having asked the rider to secure the horse's head, several strongmen pulled slowly but surely on the lunge line. To my relief, the horse then raised itself and stood up. It appeared to be none the worse for its fall and since it was "winded", a short period of rest was required prior to the journey home. The same procedure was undertaken on the second and third horse with a similar outcome.

However, the fifth and last horse was in a different category. It was a black mare with a blaze and four socks, together with a distinctive "Prophets Thumb" depression on its lower left neck. I checked her reflexes again. There was no movement in her tail and when grasped it had a flaccid feel. There was no movement in her hind legs. The rectal reflex was absent. She was looking anxiously at her flank but was not making any attempt to raise herself. It very much looked as if she had broken her back. Just to be sure that she was not just winded, the mare was rolled over as already described for the other four horses, but in this instance, the mare made no attempt to raise herself. By this time, the owners had arrived and they could see that the outlook was not good. Fortunately, they had seen horses with broken banks before so they were familiar with the mare's plight. I enquired about insurance cover for death due to accident and they assured me that the mayor was covered for this eventuality. When all the other horses had left the scene of the accident, I shot her to avoid any further unnecessary suffering. I made a detailed description of her colours and markings in the traditional way since I knew that I would have to forward a certificate to the insurance company to enable the owners to make a satisfactory claim.

The courting couple

Spring had sprung and nature was coming alive again. I was called to a thoroughbred mare that was having difficulty suckling her foal. I had to meet the grooms at the stud and follow them up a rough track to the Downs, where the mares and foals had just been turned out in the paddocks on the spring grass. The clocks had just gone forward and there was a definite feeling of spring in the air.

As I was attending to the mare and foal, I was summoned over the two-way radio telephone to attend to another mare who was having difficulty foaling. When I arrived at the end of the track, I could not open the five-barred gate since, in the meantime, a minuscule Reliant Robin motorcar had parked on the downhill side. I needed to pass by urgently to attend to my emergency call. By this time it was dark. I turned off the car engine and climbed over the five-barred entrance field gate. By the light of the moon, I could see that all the car windows were "steamed up". I felt certain that there must be a courting couple inside the motorcar. I knocked on the windows, one after the other, but there was no response. What was I to do? I returned to my car since I

had heard the two-way radio trying to communicate with me again. The receptionist said that she had had Mrs McCorquodale on the telephone again, wondering how long I would be since the mare was having major problems foaling. "The access trackway is blocked by a Reliant Robin, the windows are all steamed up so I assume that there must be a courting couple inside. I will see what I can do to speed things up." I turned on the car engine, rapidly flashed the headlights several times and tooted the horn repeatedly. "I can't seem to shift them!" I said to the secretary, in desperation. "I will try knocking on the car windows again." I left my headlights on and the car engine running to enable me to see what I was doing. This time I brought my powerful torch with me in case I needed it. I climbed over the five-barred gate, yet again. I walked around the Reliant Robin knocking on all the windows in turn, with increasing intensity. I tried to open the doors but they were all securely locked. "This is private property. I urgently need to drive through, since I have been summoned to an urgent call and you are blocking my way." There was still no response. I turned on my strong torch and shone the light through the windows. It was impossible to see anything since the steam on the windows had somewhat intensified.
A voice from the depths suddenly said: "Hang on mate, whilst I get my trousers on!" At last, I had received the first indications of life from inside the minute motorcar. I would have to bide my time but at least I had something to placate not only the practice receptionist but also the persistent Mrs McCorquodale. This was the last and sole statement that emanated from inside this celebrated little motorcar. The next thing I heard was the Reliant Robin engine starting up, as the handbrake was rapidly released, before it reversed precariously down the slope with no sign of either head lights or tail lights. Now that the miniature car had done a complete U-turn on three wheels, the headlights were hurriedly turned on as it sped away down the trackway in a perilous manner.
With my path unblocked by this unorthodox obstruction, I opened the five-barred gate, returned to my motorcar and reassured the long-suffering practice receptionist (who was standing by patiently waiting for a response from the two-way radio) that I was finally on my way.
Off to pastures new
The practice offered me a partnership. Major Crawshaw was employed by a large Bloodstock Agency and frequently attended the sales at Ascot, Doncaster and Newmarket. The partners wanted a further equine partner to cover for him in his absence. I was honoured and flattered to be offered the opportunity of a partnership on the equine side of a rapidly expanding and successful practice. I had not long qualified, had recently married and was still unsure in which part of the country I wanted to settle. After lengthy discussions with my wife, it was decided that for the time being, it would be better for me to continue gaining valuable experience with horses. I declined their offer. The partners, understandably from their point of view, on being appraised that I was not going to accept their offer of partnership, informed me that I would have to broaden my experience elsewhere. Following their

monthly partners' meeting, it was resolved that they would advertise
for an equine assistant with view to partnership.

It so happened that one of the partners knew that a single-handed
equine vet in Badminton in Gloucestershire was on the point of
advertising for an assistant. That practice only dealt with equine
cases. It was suggested that I should apply. Two days later I
attended an interview. It was a relatively new practice. The surgery
was situated in a small purpose-built rectangular enclosed yard. It
also contained an X-ray room, treatment room, operating theatre, tack
room and a range of loose boxes. Mr Graham Grant kept his own hunters
and point-to-point racehorses in the yard, he was assisted by an ex-
Royal Army Veterinary Corps groom, called Barney - a small man about
five foot three inches tall who wore his cap at a jaunty angle. Mr
Graham Grant, affectionately known to his friends as GG (gee gee), was
a tall, distinguished-looking gentleman. He asked my professional
opinion on a series of horses stabled in the loose boxes.

A short time later he telephoned to say that he had interviewed fifteen
veterinary surgeons (equine practices were very popular in those days)
and that I was on a short list of two, he invited me to bring my wife
for dinner. I soon discovered over dinner, that he was a charming
person, a wonderful storyteller with an endless list of tales. These
went on into the small hours and in due course I was offered the job.
Major Crawshaw asked me to stay on for a period of time until the
practice had found a replacement assistant. The practice asked me to
introduce my successor to the clients. This was all part of the
amicable agreement between the two practices. By mutual agreement, I
started my new post two months later.

The Beaufort Hunt

The practice accommodation was an enchanting refurbished millhouse in a nearby village in the Cotswolds. The breakfast room was high up on the side of the millhouse with a window overlooking the river. It was a delight to see the blue-green flash of the kingfisher swooping under the adjacent bridge as it worked the stream hunting for fish.

An Irish vet looks back
by Fergus Ferguson ©

The rolling countryside of the south Cotswolds was charming,
particularly the endless network of drystone walls surrounding the
fields and edging the lanes. The 10th Duke of Beaufort owned nearly
all the land in the district. Most of the farmers were his tenants.
The countryside was totally unspoiled. The cottages were delightful.
They were all made of local Cotswold stone, well weathered by an
accumulation of lichen over the years. This gave the cottages their
unique mellow yellow colour. Many of them had mullioned windows, they
were all roofed with large cut stone slab tiles, quarried locally. It
was ideal hunting country - undulating fields where the horses could
gallop for miles. Many city dwellers hunted with the Beaufort and kept
their horses at livery in the area. It was not uncommon to see 200-300
mounted particularly on a Saturday. The Wednesday country was also
very popular.

The Duchess of Beaufort

Mr Grant told me that he did a lot of work with hunters and racehorses
- mainly Point-to-Point and National Hunt racehorses. The workload was
divided between a local horse practice, within a thirty-mile radius of
Badminton, and a consultancy equine practice in the West Country in
Somerset, Dorset, Devon and Cornwall. An assistant was needed to look
after the local horses during his monthly peripatetic long distance
calls in the West Country.

My very first job was to visit the stables at Badminton House - a
Palladian mansion and the home of the Dukes of Beaufort since the 17th
century. The house had been extensively altered in 1740 by William
Kent. He had originally laid out the grounds but later Capability
Brown extended the landscaping. This created the magnificent effect of
the grounds around the house and was a fitting setting for the leading
hunt in the country. Before I set off, Mr Grant explained to me that
the Duke of Beaufort was affectionately known and addressed by all as
"Master". I was never quite sure whether this was because the 10th
Duke was Master of the famous Beaufort Hunt or Master of the Horse. I
suspect that it was the former.

I had an appointment at 10 o'clock to meet the stud groom to rasp
several horses' teeth. I was feeling rather nervous. I knew that the
veterinary examination always took place in the stable yard on the
third day of the world-famous Badminton Horse Trials. The appointed
panel of experts, which included a leading equine veterinary surgeon,
observed the horses being trotted up over the cobbled stones in the
yard. The purpose of this inspection is to check to see if any of the
horses are lame, having completed the dressage and the rigorous cross-
country phase on the previous two days. A horse that is lame or unfit
to compete for any reason is disqualified from participating in the
third and final phase - the show jumping. Having imagined the clip
clop of innumerable horses' feet, trotting up before the panel of
experts and heard from Major Crawshaw and other colleagues how the
inspection takes place, I felt I had a good idea about the layout and
atmosphere of the very famous yard.

As I approached Badminton House and drove in through the gates, nothing
had prepared me for the sight that met my eyes. It was the most

enchanting old-fashioned yard that I had ever visited - enclosed on three sides, with stabling on the ground floor. The grooms' living quarters were situated above the stables. This enclosure, complete with clock tower, created a wonderfully intimate, traditional atmosphere - a quintessentially English yard. As I alighted from my motor car, I felt as if I was entering a time warp. The atmosphere of the place, the smell of saddle soap and horse manure, and the sounds of the horses, all created a sense of timelessness. Everything was shipshape and Bristol fashion - a place for everything and everything in its place.

Late summer is the normal time to rasp horses' teeth ready for the forthcoming season - the horses had recently come in from grass. I entered the stable door. This opened on to an elongated room with a corridor running the full length of the building with traditional cage-style loose boxes leading off it. There was a horse standing in each loose box. I could not find the stud groom. The only person in sight was a lady, standing at the far end of the corridor. Casually dressed, she seemed to be very much at home, engaging me in conversation. I introduced myself as the new vet - Mr Grant's assistant. This charming lady welcomed me to Badminton House. I did not know who she was and was unsure what to say.

I enquired: 'Do you hunt?' She replied in a matter of fact sort of way that she did.

'How often do you hunt?' I continued.

'Two or three times a week,' she replied, and bade me good morning. The stud groom then appeared, introduced himself and we commenced rasping the horses' teeth.

I enquired of him: 'Who was that lady speaking to me, when you arrived?'

He replied: 'That was the Duchess of Beaufort, Master's wife.'

In the circumstances, I could not help seeing the incongruity of the situation, as I continued rasping the horses' teeth in silent contemplation.

Mr Grant hunted regularly, mainly with the Beaufort but occasionally with the Avon Vale and other local hunts. During his monthly tours of the West Country, he frequently fitted in a day's hunting, he was also very keen on skiing. Long periods of his absence were an ideal opportunity for me, as a young inexperienced vet, to gain more equine knowledge in specialist horse practice. Prior to coming to Badminton, I had had little experience of riding. GG's horses needed exercising. Early in the morning I rode out with Barney - an excellent horseman of the old school. However, it is one thing to trot along the lanes under the eagle eye of an experienced horseman but quite another matter to be mounted on a fit horse full of oats, when the hounds are in full cry and the field is in hot pursuit.

The Cryptorchid - 'If in doubt cut it out!'

A large two-year old liver chestnut thoroughbred Cornish colt, Polmassick, had been referred to the practice for surgery. This was what is known in the profession as a cryptorchid (crypto from the Greek <u>kruptos</u> = hidden, meaning concealed as in cryptic or crypt, orchid from

the Latin <u>orkhis</u>, originally = testicle, with reference to the shape of the orchid's tuber, ie hidden or undescended testicle) or rig, that is to say it has only one testicle descended in the scrotum. Once anaesthetised, the colt was placed on his back and supported by four bales of straw. A traditional leather hobble was attached in turn round each pastern, each being secured with a chain. Finally, they were all pulled together and anchored by the screw of a metal D-ring. Barney sat on the horse's head, he always gave a running commentary with every operation, frequently regaling me with all the details of previous veterinary disasters that he had encountered in his days with the Royal Army Veterinary Corps. Although I enjoyed Barney's stories, sometimes I found them very distracting when I was trying to concentrate. As I was attempting to work out which structure I was to sever, he told me a story about a young vet who had recently joined the Corps, he was performing a neurectomy on a horse and Barney as usual was sitting on its head. The vet was attempting to differentiate between the vein, the artery and the nerve - not an easy task in a bloodless site, with a tourniquet tightly secured. He raised one of the three structures with the blunt edge of a pair of scissors and enquired of Barney whether he thought it might in fact be the nerve. Barney, apparently, had replied jokingly, as was his wont: 'If in doubt, cut it out.'
The vet took him literally, and did so. Instantly, blood spurted hitting his spectacles. On hearing this remark, I resolved that henceforth I would take everything that Barney said with a pinch of salt. I managed to locate the minute "hidden" undescended testicle high up in the groin and remove it with the crushing and cutting action of the emasculator. Finding the retained testicle was quite a relief since it is frequently difficult to locate due to its small size and proximity to major blood vessels. By contrast, the removal of the large descended testicle was straightforward.
Apart from the risk of taking Barney literally, he was a wonderful character and a good help to me in Mr Grant's absence. He had been Col Pelham's batman in the Veterinary Corps during the War and had gained vast surgical experience in remount depots in North Africa by assisting and serving Col Pelham. When Col Pelham was demobbed, he invited Barney to join him in his recently established veterinary practice in the Cotswolds. The Colonel became one of the leading equine surgeons in the country. In due course, Barney joined Mr Grant's practice in Badminton, he was a very useful asset to any veterinary practice.
I was now becoming passionately interested in horse practice and I had definitely decided to try to make it my career. However, sometimes fate intervenes in a peculiar way, frequently beyond one's control. I was very sad to leave Badminton and the Beaufort Hunt.

Llanfihangel Wells

Horse practices were still few and far between. I needed a continuing
source of income quickly. A single-handed farm animal vet was

An Irish vet looks back
by Fergus Ferguson ©

advertising in the Veterinary Record for a locum at Llanfihangel Wells
in mid Wales. There was no going away on holiday, his need for a locum
was twofold: firstly, the volume of his work increased dramatically in
the springtime, secondly, and more importantly, he had been unable to
cope with many of the routine procedures in the practice, in particular
castration of the local Welsh black cattle. I was asked if I would be
willing to castrate the vast numbers which still remained entire and I
agreed to spend a few weeks helping him catch up. Apart from one
month's experience at an outward-bound camp as a schoolboy in
Aberystwyth, I had never been to Wales. I was very much looking
forward to the opportunity.
It was springtime, the ewes were lambing and the countryside was coming
alive again after the long winter sleep. The scenery in the Welsh
hills is magnificent. The wooded slopes leading down to the upper
reaches of the river Wye in the valley are beyond compare. Mr Elwyn
Llewellyn had a very busy practice. It was a large stock rearing area
- beef cattle and sheep.
Elwyn always made arrangements with a local hotel in the Spa town to
accommodate his locums. When I arrived at the hotel, after my long
journey from Badminton, the owner, Mrs Bronwyn Davies, greeted me. Mr
Llewellyn had told me that she was passionately interested in singing
and sang regularly in the local choir, she was a contralto who
participated in the regional and national Eisteddfods. Mrs Davies first
language was Welsh, since she came from Blaenau Ffestiniog in North
Wales, her other passion was cooking - she had trained as a Cordon-bleu
chef and I was reliably informed that I would be extremely well fed
throughout my stay.
 Mrs Davies greeted me like a long-lost friend and made me feel very
welcome. Larger than life, a charismatic lady who seemed as if she
would be great fun at a party. To this day I remember her well, framed
in the doorway of her hotel, and can still hear her warm, lilting Welsh
voice ringing in my ears, she invited me to fetch my belongings and
showed me to my room on the second floor.
'You must be weary after your long journey. Would you care for a pot
of tea? Dinner will not be served until eight o'clock. Make yourself
at home and come down to the sitting room in ten minutes. I will have
a pot of tea waiting for you. There are daily newspapers and magazines
in there for guests to read.'
A few minutes later I found my way downstairs. Bronwyn was waiting for
me.
'Come into the sitting room.'
A welcome pot of tea, some freshly cut sandwiches and delicious-looking
home-made walnut cake made me realise how hungry I was.
'We have six other guests tonight. I will introduce you later. They
are all still at work. If you would like a drink before your meal, my
husband will be around to serve you after six o'clock.'
Bronwyn excused herself and bustled off to the nether regions of the
hotel. As I sat enjoying my afternoon tea, I contemplated my
surroundings. The well-proportioned, high-ceilinged room was
pleasantly decorated with an eclectic mix of carefully chosen

An Irish vet looks back
by Fergus Ferguson ©

paintings. This created a wonderfully relaxed ambience. The large
sliding-sash windows were elegantly dressed with floor length, fully-
lined traditional William Morris print curtains, partially hiding the
substantial wooden shutters, neatly folded back into the window recess.
The chairs and sofas were comfortable and inviting. I tried to imagine
what the house might have been like before it became a hotel. In my
mind's eye I could just picture great uncle Hubert, having enjoyed an
invigorating day's fishing on the river Wye, taking a postprandial nap,
after consuming a hearty five-course meal, all washed down with a
copious amount of wine, followed by a glass or two of port.
The hotel definitely exuded a feeling of an interesting past. The
imagination could run wild. The four-panelled doors, complete with
ornate finger-plates, original porcelain handles and keyholes,
portrayed an air of elegant living. The large, square entrance hall
with its multi-coloured Victorian tiles and elegant staircase, was
tastefully furnished with antiques. A gleaming brass gong was sitting
purposefully on top of a highly polished substantial oak chest. I
later learned that the delightful mellow tone of the gong summoned the
guests for dinner each evening.
Sweetbreads
When I returned to the hotel the following evening, Bronwyn appeared
and enquired how I had fared at Brynfor Evans' Farm at Maesmynis.
'Brynfor has been patiently awaiting your arrival. Elwyn is really
behind with his routine work. Brynfor sings with me in the choir. We
meet quite regularly at rehearsals. I have known the family for
years.'
Normally everything that passes between veterinary surgeon and client
is confidential and should not be disclosed to a third party. However,
since Bronwyn knew precisely where I had been and what I had been
doing, it seemed pointless to even consider such professional niceties.
'I expect you will return there again tomorrow, Fergus. Brynfor thinks
it will take you several days to finish the job.'
I nodded in agreement.
'Would you be willing to do me a favour, Fergus? To save a journey, if
I speak to Brynfor this evening, and he places the testicles in
buckets, would you be willing to bring them back here? They are
absolutely delicious properly prepared as a hors-d'oeuvre on toast.'
I agreed.
'When you have finished, drive around to the back of the hotel and I
will be waiting for you at the kitchen door.'
As I drew up in the farmyard next morning, Brynfor Evans was just
coming out of the scullery door of the farmhouse, clutching several
large galvanised metal buckets. These looked as if they had been
meticulously scrubbed and cleaned, he was grinning from ear to ear. It
was obvious from his demeanour that he was only too pleased to be able
to assist his good friend Bronwyn.
'Mrs Evans has cleaned these up especially for you. Now you can fill
them to the brim for Bronwyn.'
I continued to castrate the bull calves, rapidly filling the
conveniently placed receptacles. At the end of the day, Mr Evans

An Irish vet looks back
by Fergus Ferguson ©

assisted me enthusiastically to load the overflowing buckets into
various parts of my car. Assuring me that Bronwyn was an excellent cook
and that in due course the testicles would taste delicious.
That evening, on my return from the farm, instead of parking in the
usual place in the street, I drove around to the back of the hotel to
the kitchen door. True to her word, Bronwyn was waiting for me,
delighted to see that I had brought her several bucketsful of
testicles. Eagerly she helped me unload them from my motor car. Out of
the corner of my eye I could see that one of the guests was watching us
intently from an upstairs sash window which overlooked the backyard.
The following evening all the guests were assembled in the sitting
room. It was an exclusively male group - a mixture of business and
professional men. I could see from the large number of assembled
guests, that the hotel was filled to capacity. The gong sounded in the
hallway at 8.00pm sharp, announcing dinner. All the guests moved into
the adjacent dining room and sat down around the large rectangular
table. This huge table occupied the entirety of the small dining room.
Mrs Davies entered through the double swing doors bearing a large tray
full of plates. The individual steaming plates were deftly distributed
to each guest. Strips of meat had been neatly arranged on small
rectangles of hot buttered toast, flavoured with salt and pepper, one
small plate for each guest. The smell was wonderful. The guests
devoured the offering with obvious delight. Everyone agreed that it
had tasted delicious. An ideal hors-d'oeuvre with which to commence a
meal.
The gentleman on my left had been extolling the virtues of Bronwyn's
cooking generally and waxing lyrical about the delicacies of the hors-
d'oeuvre in particular. Charles Houghton-Browne was a bank inspector
and I knew from the conversation that I had had with him on the
previous evening that he regarded himself as something of a gourmet. I
could see from the puzzled look on his face that he was frantically
trying to ascertain what it was that we had just eaten, but I
instinctively felt, even with his extensive knowledge as a connoisseur,
he would be unable to do so.
'Does anyone know the contents of Bronwyn's surprise hors-d'oeuvre?' he
enquired, tentatively.
Silence prevailed. Eventually the gentleman, who had been watching me
across the table, exclaimed: 'What was in all those metal buckets which
I saw you and Bronwyn unloading from your motorcar last night? You
took them straight into Bronwyn's kitchen.'
I felt that the cat was out of the bag! Bronwyn's timely entrance to
collect the plates saved me from having to answer a difficult and
embarrassing question.
'Did you enjoy your hors-d'oeuvre, gentlemen?' she asked with a wry
smile.
To a man, everyone agreed that the hors-d'oeuvre had been delicious -
an overwhelming culinary success. I noticed that Charles had become
very quiet, he was not his usual ebullient self. All his exuberance
had deserted him. Each night, up to this point in time, he had enjoyed
showing off his knowledge of food and wine, almost to the point of

becoming a bore. He held himself out as an authority on all culinary matters and had obviously stayed at the hotel on many previous occasions. However, this time he was perplexed, to say the least, and was looking paler by the second, his usual ruddy complexion had completely changed. Before Bronwyn had a chance to answer, he stood up abruptly, clutching his napkin to his face, made a beeline for the dining-room door and left the room like a bolted fox.

The assembled guests were flabbergasted. It was obvious to everyone that poor Charles was rather squeamish. The peculiar thing about this particular episode was that Charles had no idea what he had actually eaten but his mind must have been working overtime. The thought that I might possibly have had something to do with the ingredients of the hors-d'oeuvre had made his bank inspector's brain go into overdrive.

Bronwyn said, 'Who would have guessed that Charles of all people, a self-styled gourmet, would react in this way. In all the twelve years that he has been coming to stay here, I have never known Charles to leave the table before the end of the meal, let alone in such a dramatic fashion. It is not the first time that I have given him sweetbreads to eat.'

Pendragon

The next day I returned to see Brynfor Evans at Maesmynis to continue castrating the large numbers of Welsh Black bulls. By late morning we had finished the last one. As usual, Brynfor invited me to come into the farmhouse to join the family for lunch. Sitting around the farmhouse kitchen table, following a substantial meal of Welsh lamb, roast potatoes and vegetables, Brynfor suddenly said: 'Fergus, I'd like to ask a favour of you, please.'

Over coffee I discovered the nature of the request. A large 3 year old colt had been running wild on the hills, but he was now starting to make a nuisance of himself with the mares next door.

Brynfor suddenly declared: 'Will you castrate him for us, Fergus? His name is Pendragon. There is plenty of help on the farm. We will soon drive him into the barn for you when you have finished your coffee. I have asked Elwyn many times to attend to him. Elwyn looked at him once when he was here visiting another animal, but he always seems to be so busy. You have done such a good job with the bulls, I am sure everything will be fine.'

I had a sneaking suspicion that everything would be far from fine. 'Is he halter-broken, Brynfor?' I tentatively enquired.

'Well, not really. We did manage to catch him once or twice when he was a foal, but he is so big and strong. We had hoped to have him broken in by now, but we have been so busy on the farm with the lambing, we just haven't had time.'

'Don't you think he should be halter-broken first?' I enquired, thinking that this might be a possible way out for me.

'Yes, you're right Fergus, in an ideal world. The problem is, if we wait any longer he may break out and cover my neighbour's mares. They are all valuable thoroughbreds and he would not be very happy if he discovered that they were in foal to my colt, he's not exactly a Derby winner, so there would be a fearful fuss. Anyway, Bronwyn told me that you are very keen on horses, and that you are hoping to specialise in equine practice. This would be an ideal opportunity for you to gain some experience with my chap.'

I could feel myself being inveigled into agreeing to castrate Pendragon, which I instinctively knew would be no sinecure. My suspicions had proved correct. As we drove this unbroken colt off the hills into the barn, I could see straight away that he was not used to being handled. His eyes were protruding with terror. Pendragon was a dark bay colt with a much exaggerated, high-stepping action, his crest was already extremely well developed and he had a long, flowing mane. I knew that testosterone (the male sex hormone) had been pumping through his veins for some long time. Wild as a Spanish fighting bull. Somehow we would have to get a halter on to his head in order to try to control him. I suddenly remembered the old trick which I had learnt from the gypsies at Winterbourne Monachorum.

'Do you perchance have a long bamboo cane, Brynfor?' I asked. Fortunately, Mrs Evans was a very keen gardener and kept a large supply of ten-foot long canes for her runner beans. I slipped the pole piece of my rope halter, double-looped, through the tendered bamboo pole.

'Now drive him along the wall and I will see if I can manoeuvre my halter on to his head.'

I strategically attached my rope halter to the end of the bamboo pole. Just as Pendragon was passing me, I held the straight pole in front of his nose and managed to secure his muzzle with the lower part of the halter. Using the long cane, I quickly jerked the pole piece of the rope halter behind his ears. I pulled the bamboo pole away at the critical moment and, in a flash, I had the rope halter attached to his head. So far, so good, I thought. I knew from previous experience that this was the easy bit. Now the fun would really start!

As soon as Pendragon felt the halter pulling on his head, he panicked, he bolted towards the half door that was open at the top. Fortunately, I had tied a lunge line to the shank of the rope halter.

'Come on everyone, grab the lunge line as quickly as you can, but watch he doesn't kick you with his hind legs.'

I could see from his agitated behaviour that he was absolutely terrified. Suddenly he reared up in an attempt to escape through the open part of the half door; he could see the fields and freedom across the yard in the valley below. Once he realised that there was no escape through the half door (fortunately it was securely bolted), he started pulling on the lunge line, as he careered at a brisk trot around the walls of the large barn, and his behaviour was exactly as I had anticipated.

'Just let him run around the walls and eventually the lunge line will shorten, as it winds around the solid oak post in the middle of the barn. Once he reaches the end of his tether, I will have to inject a tranquilliser into the jugular vein in his neck to calm him down.'

I pulled the end of the lunge line around the solid oak post, about four feet above the cobbled floor, calling on the men to come and help.

'One of you keep driving him on, but don't get too close to his hind legs,' I said, as I reiterated the safety warning. This was the type

105

of situation where prompt action was required by everyone. Fortunately all the helpers were experienced stockmen and well aware of the danger. Eventually, Pendragon could go no further, he stopped struggling as his head neared the end of the shank of the rope halter, and he was scared stiff. This was my opportunity. I promptly stepped forward and injected the sedative into his jugular vein. A short time later the tranquilliser began to take affect. Pendragon started to calm down. Now that he had relaxed slightly, local anaesthetic was injected (with considerable difficulty) into each testicle.

Once the local anaesthetic had taken affect, I started the operation. In the mid sixties, the tranquillisers then available were not very affective. Pendragon was extremely apprehensive and still disliked being handled. I was rapidly beginning to wish that I had stuck to my guns and followed my instincts. I should have insisted that Pendragon was properly halter-broken and regularly handled, prior to any attempt at castration. So many times in veterinary practice I found myself in the selfsame situation where one was persuaded to do things against one's better judgement. It was probably something to do with one's training at university, empathising with the owner's plight, and a desire to help. There was no turning back.

Having carefully washed and disinfected the scrotum I grasped the scalpel, together with its attached scalpel blade, from inside the metal steriliser. I positioned myself with my back to Pendragon's near side flank, grasped his off side testicle in my left hand, and made a bold incision through the scrotal skin. The well-developed testicle dropped down through the incision in the scrotum making it readily accessible for removal. The scalpel and its blade were replaced in the steriliser and exchanged for the gleaming, stainless steel emasculator. The drooping testicle was secured in my left hand, twisted, and pulled to its full extent, to enable me to attach the emasculator around the spermatic cord as high up in the groin as possible. I then squeezed the handles of the emasculator with my right hand, as quickly and firmly as I could. The simultaneous crushing and cutting action of the cleverly designed emasculator worked like a dream. The huge testicle dropped on the bed of straw just between Pendragon's hind legs. The handles of the emasculator were kept tightly squeezed for as long as possible in order to crush the well-developed spermatic blood vessels, thereby minimising postoperative haemorrhage. I released my grip on the emasculator handles and removed the instrument from Pendragon's groin. There was no evidence of haemorrhage or prolapse of the intestines. I breathed a sigh of relief. So far so good. I felt that, having removed one testicle successfully, I was half way there! With my confidence increasing, I then braced myself as I commenced the removal of the remaining testicle. I made a confident incision in the near side of Pendragon's scrotum. The testicle appeared through my incision as expected. However, just as I turned around to grasp the emasculator (my concentration wavered for a split second), Pendragon moved his hind quarters towards me, took aim and kicked me with his near hind foot, at full pelt, on the inside of my right shin. It was an extremely powerful blow. I was unsure whether or not my leg was

An Irish vet looks back
by Fergus Ferguson ©

broken. The pain was excruciating. Despite the agony, I could still
bear some weight on my injured leg.
'How are you, Fergus?' enquired Brynfor, with genuine concern. 'Have
you broken your leg? Would you like me to call a doctor?'
I was not the type of person to throw in the towel at the first sign of
trouble. It was instilled into me at an early age by my father, and
later on by the instructors at the Outward Bound School. Carry on,
come what may. Stiff upper lip, come hell or high water.
'I expect I'll be all right in a minute or two. We'll finish the job
first. My leg can wait 'til later,' I said, putting a brave face on
it. Once I had recovered from the shock of the sudden, violent but not
unexpected kick, I picked up the emasculator and approached Pendragon
once more. Fortunately, I managed to complete the operation without
further incident.
'Come indoors, Fergus. You look as if you could do with a stiff drink.
As soon as you are ready I will drive you into the local hospital. I
feel certain that they will want to take an X-ray of your injured leg.
That was a very nasty kick indeed. Let me help you.'
I placed my arm around Brynfor's broad shoulders, using his powerful
frame to support my injured limb. As I hobbled into the farmhouse
kitchen, Mrs Evans looked most concerned. Brynfor poured me a large
whisky.
'Here, Fergus. Drink this. It will help ease the pain. I will
telephone the local hospital to let them know what has happened. I
have known the theatre sister for years. You will be in safe hands,
she is a soprano and sings in the choir with Bronwyn. We will be on
our way as soon as you have finished your drink.'
I began to develop the distinct impression that, in this neck of the
woods, if one had friends who sang in the local choir, doors would
automatically open.
Sister Davies
A short time later, seated in the passenger seat of their solid
Landrover, I was wending my way down the hillside in the safe custody
of Mr and Mrs Evans. The large medicinal whisky was starting to take
affect and the pain was slightly less severe. Mrs Evans insisted on
wrapping me in a thick, woollen, tartan rug even though it was a mild
spring day. It will help combat the shock, she kept saying.
When we arrived at the local cottage hospital, we were greeted by a
reception party led by the singing sister. 'Sister Thomas, I would
like you to meet our locum vet, Fergus Ferguson. As you know he has
had a very bad kick on the shin, he is in a really bad way.'
Sister Thomas greeted me with both hands clasped across her well-
proportioned chest. Her impish grin seemed to say "And what on earth
have you been up to this time, young man?" She looked the type of lady
who might well be the spark who ignites the party. I felt that I was
indeed in safe hands.
Introductions over, I hobbled into the Hospital. I was shown into an
empty cubicle and instructed to lie down on the bed. A screen was
drawn around me. Sister Thomas removed my trousers. A huge black and
blue swelling had developed on my shin.

107

An Irish vet looks back
by Fergus Ferguson ©

'You have probably broken your leg, Fergus. Pendragon is big and
strong, he would have given you quite a kick. Don't put any weight on
your leg until Mr Lloyd-Griffiths has examined you, he is our local
surgeon and will be along to see you shortly.'
In due course Mr Lloyd-Griffiths with Sister Thomas and her entourage
in close attendance, came to examine me. An enormous man with jet
black hair, Mr Lloyd-Griffiths fixed me with penetrating eyes. I heard
later that he had played in the second row of the scrum for Wales. I
was hoping that it would not be necessary for him to palpate my injured
tibia. Thankfully it was not.
'I think Sister could be right. With such a forceful whack, you may
well have sustained a hairline fracture of the tibia. We had better
take an X-ray to see what has happened to you,' he opined, in a
confident manner.
By this time my shin was swollen up like a balloon. I was beginning to
think that they might be right. Sister Thomas and the junior nurses
gently rolled me onto the trolley and wheeled me into the X-ray room.
As I lay on the trolley waiting for the X-rays to be developed I began
to wonder what would happen to me if I had indeed broken my leg. I had
just arranged two further locums, to follow on immediately after I had
finished at Llanfihangel Wells; the first in a mixed practice in
Cornwall, the second in a horse practice in the Midlands. I was
particularly anxious to return to horse practice. There were few
opportunities to do so. I had hoped that this sudden accident had not
jeopardised my career. Lying flat out on the trolley, I could feel
myself drifting into a soporific state (Sister Thomas had given me an
injection to relieve the pain). I did not think it would have been
politic to inform her beforehand that Brynfor had already given me a
stiff whisky! Sister Thomas' injection, combined with the affects of
the whisky, knocked me for six. As I slowly nodded off, my mind began
to drift back to my childhood days in Ireland. In no time I was
asleep.

Boyhood stories

<u>Belfast zoo</u>

When I was a small boy, aged about eight years of age, my mother took me on a visit to Belfast zoo. I was fascinated by all the animals. I had never seen many of the animals before. Eventually, we arrived at the monkey enclosure. I was holding onto the perimeter wire cage looking at some monkeys perched upon a tree. Suddenly, one of the monkeys scuttled down the tree, sprang towards me grabbing my spectacles. Running away at lightning speed, re-climbed the tree, together with my spectacles. My mother was distraught since, being short-sighted, I needed my spectacles to enable me to see properly. Mother immediately brought this to the attention of one of the animal keepers, who was most concerned. Eventually, the keeper inveigled the monkey into descending from his perch by the offer of some bananas. This wheeze worked and the keeper managed to retrieve my spectacles, returning them to me, fortunately intact.

The birds and the bees

'Daddy, what's the difference between a bull and a bullock?' I enquired, innocently. To this day, I have been unable to work out what possessed me to ask such a question of my father, especially at that precise moment. It was all just part of growing up. I did not know it at the time, but this was probably the early stirring of my developing interest in animals and my desire to become a practising veterinary surgeon.

It was in the early part of the Fifties. I was a small boy - just a slip of a lad - aged twelve years. Every summer my family spent their annual holiday in the same small village on the shores of Carlingford Lough at the foot of the Mourne Mountains in County Down, Ireland. The scenery was magnificent. The Mourne Mountains were the inspiration for the world famous song and evocative melody: "Where the mountains of Mourne sweep down to the sea".

The family always swam every afternoon come rain, hail, or shine. On this particular July day, the sea was freezing cold. Finn MacCool, the mountain Giant, was lying on the other side of the glistening water of the Lough. Provided you were standing in the right place, you could see the contours of the Giant's forehead, as he lay asleep: eyes, nose, mouth, and chin. There is a tradition of folklore in Ireland, where stories are passed from generation to generation by word of mouth. Every boy learned all about these myriad giants and their antics, at their father's knee.

After the swim, I was covered in goose pimples, shivering and blue with cold. I was frantically trying to dry myself with a towel, whilst hopping from foot to foot on the unforgiving pebble beach. Inquisitive from an early age, I consulted my father when I was unsure about something. Curiously, he had still not answered my enquiry; I knew by

109

the look on my father's face that it was, from his perspective, different from my normal, naive questions.

When he was a boy, matters appertaining to sex and sex education, were not on the parental agenda. They were taboo subjects. The post-war era changed these anachronistic attitudes. Euphemisms about storks and gooseberry bushes were no longer acceptable. Parents were now under a duty to address such troublesome issues. My father's time had come. Would he fail in his parental duty? He was a typical product of his background and generation: born in Edwardian times, a banker by profession, conservative by nature, from a very strict Methodist background. A dark cloud had descended over his face. Was this the dreaded moment that he had been waiting for?

For two long hours, in the freezing cold, clad only in swimming trunks, I was led along nettle-covered lanes, forced to climb over five-barred gates and under barbed wire fences, to view innumerable bovines: cows, calves, heifers, bulls, and bullocks. All was revealed. Nothing was overlooked. Everything was shown and pointed out. Following this cross-country expedition, suffice it to say I was none the wiser and certainly never, ever raised the subject again.

Some 60 years later, following a lifetime practising as a veterinary surgeon in Ireland, England and Wales, and about 20 years into my retirement, I realised how much I missed all the contact with people and their animals. People have strange ways and use quaint expressions. Peculiar but interesting things happen to a vet.

Around the Millennium the idea crystallised in my mind when I was flying off, at short notice, to visit my Irish mother who was then ninety-two years old, whose health was failing. I had booked a last minute flight via Exeter. The somewhat old-fashioned rural Devon airport had scarcely changed in 35 years. There was no coach to take one to the little aeroplane, sitting forlornly on the tarmac in the brilliant sunshine. I climbed to the top of the flight of steps, and paused briefly to view the antiquated aircraft, whilst leaning on my trusty blackthorn thumbstick.

'How old is the old girl?' I enquired of the Air Stewardess (une femme d'un certain age), who was smiling benignly as she welcomed everyone on board the flight. Her face fell. Immediately, I realised that my question had been misunderstood. I could see that she was crestfallen. Fearing anything I might say or do would inevitably exacerbate an already delicate situation, I knew I was in yet another jam with no easy way of extricating myself. Fortunately, my partner, who was all too familiar with my countless gaffes, solecisms, indiscretions and blunders, came to my rescue.

She was acutely aware of the impasse and the lady's discomfiture, reassuring her by saying, 'He's asking you about the age of the aeroplane!'

Instantly, the smile returned to her face. Regaining her composure, she retorted, 'Not as old as she looks!' Honour was saved. In a trice, she deftly arrested my thumbstick and stowed it securely at the back of the aeroplane, before showing us to our seats. This incident was the catalyst that stimulated me to start writing my veterinary anecdotes.

Chepstow

Chepstow racecourse

The principal of the practice was one of the honorary veterinary surgeons at Chepstow racecourse, he took his duties very seriously. Driving around the outside of the racecourse in his Land Rover. It was a very bumpy ride. I had not been in Chepstow very long when I was invited to attend one of the race meetings as honorary veterinary surgeon. I was in attendance with a colleague from one of the adjacent practices. The vet is always given a circular badge marked honorary veterinary surgeon, so that owners, trainers and the general racing public know who he is.

Compared to modern mandatory requirements, I did not have sufficient experience to do the job properly but for practical reasons, I was thrown in at the deep end. It was National Hunt racing and the going was good to firm. Suddenly, one of the horses was in trouble right in front of the stands. It had been travelling at high speed and was abruptly "on three legs." It seemed to have sustained a spontaneous fracture of one of the bones in its front legs and the outlook was not very good. On these occasions, inevitably a large crowd is milling around (usually out of curiosity) and it is very difficult to carry out a clinical examination in such circumstances. I suggested that the horse should be taken to a nearby loose box that was used exclusively for such examinations. It seemed to me that the horse had sustained a major fracture of one of the large bones of the shoulder joint - either the humerus or the scapula. Fortunately, the trainer had suddenly appeared so I had someone in a position of authority in which to consider the position. I was definitely of the opinion that the horse should be put out of its misery since any orthopaedic surgery seemed out of the question. However, in these situations it is always better to suggest getting a second opinion.

I asked the other attending veterinary surgeon if he would be willing to give me an opinion on the case. He was an experienced practising veterinary surgeon and had much more experience of these tragic situations than me. He was also of the opinion that the horse should be "put down". Fortunately, the trainer agreed to this course of action. I

112

knew that euthanasia was not going to be easy since the horse was constantly moving due to severe pain. I had the help of the trainer and an experienced groom. Initially, a few horses had to be relocated from nearby loose boxes since I did not want them to be frightened by the sound of the gun. Enquiries revealed that the horse was insured but it was essential that euthanasia was carried out as soon as possible. I managed to persuade everybody to leave this unfortunate duty to the experienced groom and myself. When I had loaded a bullet into the gun, I had to wait for the right moment when the horse's head was stationary before I pulled the trigger. For an instance, the horse stopped moving from side to side; I grasped the opportunity and pulled the trigger. The horse dropped down dead. Arrangements were made to transport the horse to the local hunt kennels where a post-mortem examination could be carried out in due course.

In these sad occasions, frequently the public do not understand that shooting a horse is the most efficient, practical and humane way to perform euthanasia. Although an overdose of barbiturates could be given, the difficulty presented then is that the carcass cannot be consumed by foxhounds (particularly the horse's liver), since they would either die from barbiturate poisoning or more probably go to sleep for a couple of days; neither situation is acceptable. Even if some wonderful orthopaedic operation is carried out, the horse will immediately try to stand, but it will be unable to bear weight. Furthermore, unless a horse completely recovers from such an operation, it is pointless unless the horse is no longer lame, since no one wants a slightly lame horse.

Later in the day, I carried out a post-mortem examination on the horse. Its humerus (the large bone that makes up the lower part of the shoulder joint) was broken into over a dozen pieces. In a situation like this, it is always a relief to know that the correct decision had been made. I telephoned the trainer who was very understanding. I said that I would be willing to provide the necessary veterinary certificate for the owner if an insurance claim was going to be made.

A few days later, I received a very pleasant letter from the trainer (I think he trained in the Wantage area in Oxfordshire), thanking me for my attention.

The M4 motorway obstruction

I was summoned in the middle of the night to attend six showjumpers in a large horse transporter since the vehicle had suddenly stopped abruptly as if the brakes had seized. It was not immediately apparent to the driver what exactly had happened. It was pitch black. The vehicle was stationary and was partially blocking the motorway. I managed to drive along to the scene of the emergency. By the light of a strong torch, I ascertained that one of the horses had put its hind leg through the floor of the horse transporter and in its attempt to free itself, it had fractured the other hind leg at the hip. Clearly, the horse was going to have to be put out of its misery. However, this could not be done safely with five other horses in close proximity. I knew the farmer (and landowner) who lived quite near the scene of the accident and thought that he might be willing to help. He had some

113

boxes that could be used as temporary stabling for the five horses. The farmer was contacted and he agreed to help. Once it was determined that it was safe to do so, the five horses were led to the farm and safely placed in some temporary stabling. This simplified the situation considerably. I shot the horse with a handheld pistol and bullet. It was then possible to examine the situation and try to establish why the horse transporter had suddenly come to a dramatic stop. The wooden floor had given way and one of the horse's hind hooves had become wedged between the two tyres. It became apparent on closer inspection that the outer wheel would have to be removed before the dead horse could be taken away for disposal. The local hunt lorry was summoned and, now that the horse's hind foot had been released, the hunt lorry was able to winch the horse out of the horsebox.

Hazelbury Abbas

The snake man

A short time after arrival in Hazelbury Abbas, I received a routine call from a man who asked me if I would be willing to call to vaccinate his two cats. The only technical difficulty was that he said it would have to be an early evening call since he worked full-time in the nearby market town.

I visited at the appointed time and vaccinated his two cats. His wife very kindly offered me a drink, which I accepted. During this social interaction, John said that he had something to show me. A short time later, John returned with a large snake around his neck, writhing and wriggling consistent with the motions of a boa constrictor. I did not know the first thing about snakes since, at that time, exotic animals such as snakes were not on the veterinary curriculum. I was sitting on the sofa drinking my cup of coffee and trying to be relaxed about everything. In reality, I was extremely apprehensive since I had no idea what was coming next.

"Is it venomous?" I enquired naïvely. "No, it is not venomous. It just squeezes its prey to death." replied John, in a matter of fact manner. I could see what John meant, as I inched slightly further to my side of the sofa. "Since you have just started your veterinary practice further up the hill, I was wondering if you would be willing to take 'Sid' under your care." I was taken aback by this straightforward but reasonable request. "Of course, I will, I said nervously, provided you will be willing to help me and I can arrange for an experienced expert on snakes who would be willing to give me a second opinion if we could not sort out any problem between us." There the matter rested and during the time that I practised in Hazelbury Abbas, happily "Sid" remained healthy and free from any veterinary problems.

The intruder and the police guard dog on a winter's night

One exceedingly cold frosty February night, I retired to bed early with a hot water bottle. I was awoken abruptly by the telephone ringing at 2 a. m. My neighbour from the farm next door was in a very nervous and agitated state. An intruder had disturbed them. It was half term so they had several young people staying with them for the school vacation. Having responded to a knock on the door from a young man

115

saying that his daughter was giving birth at the local hospital and he had run out of diesel. Although suspicious, on hearing the young man's plight, my neighbour decided to offer his help. It was a clear moonlit night. On making his way across the farmyard to the barn to fetch the diesel, it was noted that the young man's vehicle was parked facing inwards in the farmhouse driveway, further alerting his suspicion. He enquired of the young man, how did it come to pass that he was parked facing inwards on a private drive and not, as would have been the norm, on the public road. Before he had time to answer, two police officers in a patrol car suddenly came round the corner. Seeing the police panicked the young man who asked not to have his presence disclosed before legging it across the farmyard with the police in hot pursuit, leaving my neighbour perplexed. A short time later, the young man re-appeared, peering in through various farmhouse windows. Fearing that he might be a threat and concerned for the children's safety, my neighbours telephoned 999 and asked for the police. Explaining that they had an intruder at the farmhouse who kept peering through the kitchen window; two police officers had appeared and had given chase around the farm. The police emergency telephonist asked for an incident number once she heard that the police were already in attendance. It was explained that they did not have an incident number since two police officers were already chasing the intruder and that this was the first time they had called the police.

In the circumstances, I was telephoned, since as a near neighbour in a small hamlet, they thought that I should be appraised of the situation. I thanked them for letting me know and asked to be kept posted. Further sleep was impossible so I went downstairs and made some tea. I could not settle. I thought I should go outside and check my own property and farm buildings. Some protection was essential in case I was attacked, so I lifted my trusty Blackthorn twitch that I used for restraining horses during my days in veterinary practice. It is a sturdy piece of Blackthorn fashioned from the hedge, with a hole drilled at one end that held a soft loop of rope that was used for placing around a horse's muzzle for restraint purposes. I put my hand through the rope loop and gripped the end of the Blackthorn twitch securely. This should act as minimum force (rather like a policeman's truncheon) just in case I was attacked. I walked quietly around the farm house and could not see any sign of an intruder. I then proceeded to check around the back of the old piggery. As I was walking around the gable end, I suddenly heard footsteps causing the hairs to rise on the back of my neck, envisaging that the intruder was just around the corner. Everything happened very quickly. Suddenly, a huge German shepherd dog on a choker chain advanced towards me, he was being restrained by a burly police sergeant that I now know was an especially trained rapid response police officer and dog handler. Dogs have a very acute sense of smell and hearing, so the dog would have been aware instantly of my presence. The adrenaline was running through my veins since I had raised the Blackthorn twitch above my head and was just about to defend myself had I been attacked. In a trice, I realised that the situation had to be rapidly defused before someone was seriously injured. "My name is

An Irish vet looks back
by Fergus Ferguson ©

Fergus Ferguson. This is my home it and is private property." Happily, the hefty police sergeant pulled the dog away from me and gave him the command to stop his attack. At the same time, I lowered my defensive wooden Blackthorn twitch with a sigh of relief. Fortunately, the expertly trained German shepherd dog had not sunk its teeth in my forearm and I had not hit the sergeant (or the dog) with my Blackthorn twitch. I dread to think what the outcome would have been had I done so.

Later that night, the young man was caught by the two police officers and taken to a police station for enquiries. I understand that he had been causing problems at a neighbouring property and may have been under the influence of drugs. His vehicle remained on my neighbour's drive for a couple of days and I now realise that it was eventually driven away by some of the young man's friends or acquaintances.

The cat in the tumble dryer

I received an emergency call from a client who said that their beloved cat "Socks", a jet black kitten, with white socks, had decided to take a nap in the tumble dryer. Unfortunately, it had been turned on with the kitten still inside. Thankfully, the dryer had not been on for too long. Socks was brought in to be checked over, and was absolutely terrified. Quite understandably, as Socks had been spinning around inside the drum at a high speed and temperature. One can only imagine what a horrifying experience this must have been for the poor kitten. His pupils were fully dilated, fur standing up stiffly up on end, resembling the metal teeth of a hair comb, as a result of adrenaline release. I gave Socks a cortisone injection and applied cool water to the skin.

Remarkably, after a few days, he had completely recovered. More than likely losing one of his nine lives. The moral of this particular story is, all cat owners should check carefully that their cat has not crawled into this warm, inviting and apparently safe hideaway within their territory. Since from their prospective, it would be only natural to enter such an inviting space and snuggle up and go to sleep.

Keep tumble dryer doors shut!

Exotic Animals

Man-eating Tigers

I took my son, aged five, to the local zoo. We saw Bengal Tigers, African elephants, monkeys and many other assorted animals. Just as our day was coming to a close, we spied an alluring little bridge going over an artificial stream. The sign above the entrance to the bridge proudly announced: "Man-eating tigers." My son was just old enough to read. I could see that he had read the sign and was keen to walk over the bridge to investigate. At the other side of the bridge, there were some man-eating tigers in cages. My son, looking me straight in the eye asked in a disarming manner: "Where is the man eating the tigers, Daddy?" From his point of view, having seen all sorts of extraordinary comings and goings at the Zoo today, a man eating a tiger would not have been too incredulous!

Windsor Safari Park, the Camel, My Car!

The autumn bank holiday was extremely nice weather, so I thought that I would treat the children to a day out at Windsor Safari Park. Unfortunately, everyone else seemed to have the same idea. The traffic was horrendous, with a long stream of cars, not only on the M4 motorway but also along the entrance to the Safari Park, resulting in one almighty jam. Everyone was becoming too warm, hungry and exceedingly restless. Eventually, we made it to the front of the queue, I paid the entrance fee and the barrier was raised. Once inside, there were many animals that were grazing on either side of the mettle carriageway. I slowed right down and put my brand spanking new Volvo car into first gear, to give the children an opportunity to view some camels at close range. Suddenly, this rather unsociable Camel, took a dislike to us, turned around and gave my new car one almighty kick with its powerful hind leg. It left a large dent in the side of my new pride and joy. Fortunately, no one was injured but my new motorcar had to have extensive bodywork. An expensive day out.

Mini-Safari in South Africa

An Irish vet looks back
by Fergus Ferguson ©

My daughter and son-in-law lived in South Africa and invited me for a short holiday near Johannesburg that included a weekend Safari expedition, since they knew that I was passionately interested in viewing wildlife at close quarters. My son thought it would be a good idea for me to fly to South Africa with him so that we could all have an African holiday. At the weekend we camped out in the bush in mainly hill country and this gave me a feeling of what Africa was really like. We were a small group of about six. I was awake every morning before dawn since I knew that this would be a once in a lifetime experience that I did not want to miss. Following some black coffee and a quick breakfast, I was transported into the bush by a Zulu driver who knew that I was very keen to see as much wildlife as possible.

It was not one of the famous wildebeest migration routes or a national park, but if one was enthusiastic, as I was, it was possible to see some of Africa's "big five." The Zulu guide pointed out everything to me. Since Leopard normally hunt at night and are secretive animals, it was unlikely that I would see one kill its prey. Since leopards frequently pull their prey up trees, so that they can escape the attentions of other hunting animals such as Lion. The Zulu guide showed me a leopard's kill that had been pulled up a tree and wedged in the branch of a tree to make consumption easier, away from the attention of other carnivores.

We stopped for lunch beside a large waterhole and saw a herd of elephant running downhill for their daily drink. They drank vast volumes of water. It was a great pleasure to see these huge African elephants and especially the way they interacted with each other. Frequently, we saw wildebeest and zebra. Early one morning, just after dawn, we passed a herd of eland. Further on, we stumbled upon a lioness and three cubs. She had focused on some kudu just over the brow of the hill and went into the crouched posture. The three cubs immediately "froze." Unfortunately, the eland must have seen or smelled her scent as they all fled in panic. The Zulu driver turned off the ignition and there was a complete "African" silence. He whispered to me that the lioness was "tucked up", since she probably hadn't eaten for several days. If she didn't kill soon, she would die and the cubs would not survive. Suddenly, the lioness turned around and advanced down the hill towards us. The window of the Land Rover on my side was open, as she passed by along the narrow track, closely followed by her cubs. The Zulu guide said that he had noticed some zebra earlier as we drove along and he thought that she was probably going to try her luck with them. Her life, and that of her cubs, was in the balance.

Aston Lucy

<u>The mouse woman</u>

I started my own veterinary practice just outside the enchanting quintessentially English North Cotswolds town of Aston Lucy. The weather was extremely hot. The town had always had the benefit of the services of a dentist and a doctor but never a practising veterinary surgeon. The family (my wife and three children) arrived amid much speculation, rumour, and gossip. What type of vet was the new arrival? Was he, perhaps, a horse vet? The substantial traditional dry stonewalls on the Cotswold Hills were wonderful for jumping. The large hedge banks, together with expansive grassland fields, were perfect for galloping, in the nearby Vale of Evesham. This was the North Cotswolds hunt country. Was the newcomer a large animal vet? Traditionally, the North Cotswolds was a stock rearing area: beef cattle and sheep. Village gossip decreed that the new vet was a dog and cat man. Many retired ex-army people living in the town, frequently owned a dog and or a cat. A small animal veterinary surgeon in their midst would be a definite asset.

It was my second day in the practice and I was very keen to make a good impression with whomever I met. I knew from previous experience that all news (both good and bad), would spread throughout any rural community like wildfire. When I returned home for lunch, my wife said that a strange woman was coming to see me early in the afternoon. The caller did not mention the nature of the consultation.

I heard the surgery doorbell ring and my wife, said, "That sounds like your afternoon appointment. I will go and have a word with her." When my wife returned, she said, "I think you had better attend soon. You have a very odd-looking client in the waiting room."

An Irish vet looks back
by Fergus Ferguson ©

Looking back on it now, this eccentric woman resembled a dishevelled Hermione Scott - Hamilton, on a bad hair day, her ruddy weather-beaten complexion revealed that she either was a countrywoman, or possessed a propensity for an occasional tipple, or both. She wore a traditional brown smock coat tightly secured with baler twine tied around her waist. Large black Wellington boots completed the picture. There were several wisps of hay entangled in her auburn alluring locks, almost certainly acquired from feeding stock of some description. She must have been a star attraction in her heyday but was definitely past her Prime.

'You must be the new vet; I will come straight to the point, since I have just turned my second field of hay,' she said nonchalantly. "I am Felicity Foxtrot - everyone knows me in Aston Lucy. As I am on my way to turn two further fields, I thought I would call in to introduce myself and enquire if you castrated mice?" This unorthodox enquiry took me aback. I had never heard of a vet performing such a procedure. I wondered how I would execute such a delicate operation. In my mind's eye, I imagined one or two mice arriving at the surgery in a cardboard box. If I had a penny for the innumerable animals that I have castrated over the years: colts, calves, lambs, piglets, goats, dogs, and cats, I would be a millionaire. Hitherto, mouse castration had never appeared on the veterinary agenda.

This prospective but unconventional client then suddenly enquired, "Do you give a discount for numbers?" This unexpected question sent me into a flat spin. I pictured this large woman advancing in a horsebox, laden down to the axles, with thousands of mice presented for castration all frantically running around the surgery floor.

My confidence was rapidly diminishing. It was time to disengage deftly from a potential professional negligence suite. I had adroitly sidestepped any reply. I felt that referring this mysterious woman to a "mouse expert" in Birmingham was the obvious way forward. I suggested that it might be a good idea if she telephoned me again in a week's time. Versed in the Art of veterinary medicine (the Science counted for very little in my modus operandi), procrastination was the traditional way to extricate oneself from a tight corner, coupled with a modicum of Irish blarney. If in doubt, do nought. Just let some water flow under the bridge. The time-honoured stratagem worked. Thankfully, that was the last I heard from this strange woman and her mice, much to my relief.

The retired Colonel and the Arsenic powders

I was asked to give a second opinion on an ageing horse. I contacted the attending veterinary surgeon to obtain authority to do so but despite several telephone calls to his surgery, I could not elicit any response. At the same time, I was being pressurised by the retired Colonel to give an opinion on his horse. Eventually, I thought the best way to proceed was to make an appointment to visit the horse in question. "Caesar" was a large, Irish flea-bitten grey horse, well over 16 hands high with a distinctive Roman nose. I could see from his incisor teeth that he was getting on in years, he had been a good servant to the Colonel but was starting to lose weight. I suspected that "Caesar" might be suffering from liver failure and perhaps it might be time for him to retire. Apparently, the attending veterinary surgeon was of a similar opinion since he had taken blood samples and had done a wide range of laboratory investigations. Surprisingly, the Colonel was mindful to have "Caesar" put down since he said that the "powders" had not done him any good. The mention of mysterious "powders" made my ears prick up. "What were these powders, please?" I said to the groom, he replied, "I will show them to you. There are just a few left in the tack room since he has been having them for weeks." On inspection, these enigmatic powders, I discovered, contained arsenic. Although many old-fashioned remedies for horses contained arsenic and were used successfully as a tonic, arsenic on its own can be extremely poisonous. Strangely, the Colonel was of a mind to send Caesar to a horse abattoir to be destroyed, thence to be exported to certain countries for human consumption. This sent alarm bells ringing. I explained to the Colonel, and the groom, that under no circumstances was the horse to be sent to this abattoir since eating the horsemeat could precipitate an outbreak of arsenical poisoning in man and even death in severe cases.

Nipper - the terrier

A young woman came to the surgery with a Jack Russell terrier, she declared: 'Mr Ferguson, I am going to be absolutely honest with you. I urgently need to put Nipper in kennels since I am going out of the country. The kennels won't accept Nipper unless he has been fully vaccinated and I have the necessary certificate signed and completed. I have tried all the local practices, so far none of them have been able to vaccinate him since he has very quick reflexes and very sharp teeth. Nipper has had many vets coming at him from all angles in an attempt at vaccination recently, he is rapidly degenerating into a nervous wreck. If you would rather not attend to him, I would quite understand.' I noticed that Nipper was wearing a substantial leather collar attached to an equally robust chain and leather lead which, to me, is always a good sign. 'I am quite happy to vaccinate Nipper if you would like to have a seat in the waiting room."

One of the first tasks I did when I arrived at Aston Lucy was to engage the services of a local carpenter to make some essential modifications. Very obligingly he screwed a large metal ring into a convenient part of the skirting board, this was ideal for handling such unconventional characters as Nipper. Fortunately, my reliable nurse Abigail was in the surgery. Abigail knew the drill and deftly slipped Nipper's lead through the metal ring and pulled tight. Nipper tried to escape from Abigail's vice-like grip but he soon realised that he was fighting a losing battle. With his head securely held beside the skirting board, it was quite simple to insert the needle (that contained the required vaccine) under his skin. Abigail completed the necessary certificate for me to sign. I felt certain that the young lady would be relieved and able to leave Nipper in the safe custody of the kennels during her trip abroad.

An Irish vet looks back
by Fergus Ferguson ©

Tales of interest

The beast of Exmoor

Peradventure, I found myself on a dairy farm on Exmoor. The farmers
also had a substantial flock of sheep that might have been the local
breed.
On arrival at the farm, just after finishing their breakfast, when all
the cows had been milked, the senior farmer informed me that they had
been visited in the night by the beast of Exmoor. As the farmers were
finishing breakfast around the farmhouse table, the oldest farmer
explained about the beast of Exmoor. I had heard about the so-called
beast of Exmoor on television and read about it in the local and
national newspapers, but was rather sceptical about its existence. I
thought that it was probably media hype. I had seen photographs in the
press that purported to show the beast of Exmoor but, with modern
photography software, a normal domestic cat could be modified to look
like a "big cat." However, the farmer's graphic description of the
situation aroused my curiosity, since he claimed that the beast of
Exmoor visited the farm every few years and usually killed and ate a
portion of one of their ewes. The farmer said that their normal
attitude towards these visits was to "hush it up", otherwise they would
be inundated by visits (or telephone calls etc.) from the local or
national media. Since I was already on the farm, he enquired if they
were under any statutory duty to report such incidents? I was unsure
what to say or do, so the farmer invited me to examine the dead ewe?
'Jump in the Land Rover, vetinree; she is lying on the grass in the
corner of a ten acre field down the lane,' he exclaimed.
The large ewe was lying on her left flank; she had huge curly horns and
a very thick fleece – probably the hardy, local Exmoor breed. The first
visually apparent abnormality was that part of her right thigh was
missing: as if it had been eaten by a wild animal such as a fox, a
rampaging domestic dog or possibly even a large wild cat. I watch many
wildlife documentary films on television and was familiar with the way
that big cats restrained their prey. Large claw marks (possibly those
of a big cat) were present on the ewe's quarters, just as if a large
cat had stalked and ambushed the ewe from behind. My attitude was
rapidly changing from one of total scepticism, regarding the existence

123

An Irish vet looks back
by Fergus Ferguson ©

of big cats, to that of being convinced by the evidence that was staring me in the face - that this was indeed the case. I knew from experience how big cats in the wild immobilised their prey, that the next part of the anatomy to be checked was the animal's throat. I immediately observed large, sharp Canine teeth had penetrated the ewe's throat and this would almost certainly have resulted in the animal's death. My attention was then drawn to the ewe's hind quarters. On one hind leg (the uppermost), all the gluteal muscles had been eaten right down to the thigh bone, and this would be a reasonable meal to satisfy the hunger of a peripatetic, marauding big cat.

I was rapidly, and dramatically, turning from "a doubting Thomas" to a firm believer in the existence of a wild or group of wild cats roaming on Exmoor. To ensure the existence, they would only need a habitat of a few thousand acres, a source of food like sheep and a place to reproduce. Exmoor would be ideal. Furthermore, the farmer confirmed my opinion, since he informed me that a local person had kept a group of wild animals (including big cats) on his premises and, according to village gossip, he had tried to sell them when he got into financial difficulties, subsequent to the introduction of the Dangerous Wild Animals Act 1976. Apparently, it was common knowledge that none of the local hauliers were willing to transport the keeper's animals, since they knew that they would never receive payment. In desperation, the keeper of the animals opened the gates of his enclosure and set all the animals free, including some big cats.

Since there are numerous flocks of sheep on Exmoor and some parts of the national park are densely afforested, it would be exceedingly difficult for anybody to see, shoot or capture a big cat.

'What's to do, vetinree?' I was beginning to believe, based on local farmers' experience, having encountered periodic deaths in their flocks of sheep that big cats did exist in the wilds of Exmoor. 'From the evidence of the two front claw marks apparent on the ewe's quarters, made by a large feline travelling in the same direction as the ewe, the sheep probably had been halted by a big cat. Knowing that big cats kill their prey by sinking their long, sharp incisor teeth into the animal's throat, it is my professional opinion that the ewe was killed by some type of big cat. The obvious absence of the gluteal muscles on the topmost part of the sheep's hind leg (eaten right down to the femur), would be sufficient meat to satisfy any ambulatory and marauding big cat.

The farmer agreed with my professional opinion. 'Have you ever seen a big cat on your farm?' I enquired. 'About three years ago, or zummat. We saw it worrying the ewes and gave chase in the Land Rover but we could not keep up with it. It then leapt right over a brook that runs down the edge of our land.' Since my curiosity was working overtime, I enquired further of the farmer, 'Do you know what type of big cat it was that you encountered?' The farmer responded that since it had a silken jet black coat, was larger than a domestic black labrador dog, was very agile, lithe and graceful, moving in a supple, fluid, and smooth fashion, they were of the opinion that it was probably a black panther. They have excellent hearing and eyesight, hunt at night and having a black coat, gives them a distinct advantage, since they are seamlessly able to stalk, ambush and kill their prey. They are secretive and mysterious animals having a long history in folklore, particularly in European witchcraft, being harbingers of good or bad luck.

Barbiturate poisoning in foxhounds

Many years ago, a story circulated amongst West Country veterinary surgeons and country people that a local pack of foxhounds had slept for a few days as a consequence of barbiturate poisoning. Fortunately none of them died. A horse had to be destroyed and that the owner was positively against having the horse shot. Consequently, the attending veterinary surgeon had no alternative, other than, to inject an overdose of long-acting barbiturate (a drug that is used for euthanasia in small animals) into the horse's jugular vein. The vet had left strict instructions with the owner that the horse should be sent to the knacker's yard and definitely not to the hunt kennels but somehow this vital piece of information was not communicated to the relevant people. In due course, the carcass was collected by the local hunt and dissected for consumption by the foxhounds. The liver, in particular, would contain a large amount of barbiturate and any foxhound eating substantial quantities of contaminated liver, is likely to be affected. Several of the foxhounds keeled over and went to sleep for two or three days.

The Wylye horse trials

I was on duty at the Wylye horse trials. I was positioned on the Yarnbury Castle hill fort, right out on the cross-country course. I was strategically positioned to deal with any accidents on the periphery of the course. All was quiet until a young man had a bad fall just beside where I was positioned. It seemed as if the horse may have broken its back. It was lying on the grass and wasn't making any effort to stand up. It had no rectal reflex, its tail was flaccid and its hind legs were not moving. The outlook was not good. I thought that the horse would have to be humanely destroyed. The rider was in a state of shock since the fall had happened very suddenly. I called for a second opinion over the radio telephone. One man walking the course had given the unhelpful opinion that the horse was "just winded" and that it would be on its feet shortly. Understandably, this raised the rider's hopes. A crowd had gathered round saying that they thought that the horse should be put out of its misery but I could not perform euthanasia without the consent of the owner/rider. Eventually, the rider could see that the situation was hopeless and gave me permission to shoot the horse. Just as I was about to do so, the horse dramatically stopped breathing. I touched its cornea and it did not blink. Its ocular mucous membranes where as white as a sheet. I could not feel a pulse or hear the heart beating when I listened with the stethoscope. There was no sign of movement. Clearly, the horse was dead, probably from internal haemorrhage. I felt very sorry for the young man. I contacted the headquarters of the event over the radio telephone and informed them of the position. Everyone was anxious to remove the horse from the course. It was a sad case.

An Irish vet looks back
by Fergus Ferguson ©

West Country (Wessex) vernacular

Advertisement that was placed in the veterinary record during a farming
recession
Yer tiz zackly,
Dunnee luk no more.
Us is lokin fir a boy,
Vit te work.

Advertisement that was placed in the veterinary record after the sex
discrimination act
'Hairy chested graduate required urgently for rapidly expanding
practice. Box number et cetera.'